I0677067

THE ESCAPE OF MR. TRIMM
HIS PLIGHT AND OTHER PLIGHTS

THE ESCAPE OF MR. TRIMM
HIS PLIGHT AND OTHER PLIGHTS

IRVIN S. COBB

TO MY WIFE

I

THE ESCAPE OF MR. TRIMM

Mr. Trimm, recently president of the late Thirteenth National Bank, was taking a trip which was different in a number of ways from any he had ever taken. To begin with, he was used to parlor cars and Pullmans and even luxurious private cars when he went anywhere; whereas now he rode with a most mixed company in a dusty, smelly day coach. In the second place, his traveling companion was not such a one as Mr. Trimm would have chosen had the choice been left to him, being a stupid-looking German-American with a drooping, yellow mustache. And in the third place, Mr. Trimm's plump white hands were folded in his lap, held in a close and enforced companionship by a new and shiny pair of Bean's Latest Model Little Giant handcuffs. Mr. Trimm was on his way to the Federal penitentiary to serve twelve years at hard labor for breaking, one way or another, about all the laws that are presumed to govern national banks.

All the time Mr. Trimm was in the Tombs, fighting for a new trial, a certain question had lain in his mind unasked and unanswered. Through the seven months of his stay in the jail that question had been always at the back part of his head, ticking away there like a little watch that never needed winding. A dozen times a day it would pop into his thoughts and then go away, only to come back again.

When Copley was taken to the penitentiary — Copley being the cashier who got off with a lighter sentence because the judge and jury held him to be no more than a blind accomplice in the wrecking of the Thirteenth National — Mr. Trimm read closely every line that the papers carried about Copley's departure. But none of them had seen fit to give the young cashier more than a short and colorless paragraph. For Copley was only a small figure in the big intrigue that had startled the country; Copley didn't have the money to hire big lawyers to carry his appeal to the higher courts for him; Copley's wife was keeping boarders; and as for Copley himself, he had been wearing stripes several months now.

With Mr. Trimm it had been vastly different. From the very beginning he had held the public eye. His bearing in court when the jury came in with their judgment; his cold defiance when the judge, in pronouncing sentence, mercilessly arraigned him and the system of finance for which he stood; the manner of his life in the Tombs; his spectacular fight to beat the verdict, had all been worth columns of newspaper space. If Mr. Trimm had been a popular poisoner, or a society woman named as co-respondent in a sensational divorce suit, the papers could not have been more generous in their space allotments. And Mr. Trimm in his cell had read all of it with smiling contempt, even to the semi-hysterical outpourings of the lady special writers who called him The Iron Man of Wall Street and undertook to analyze his emotions — and missed the mark by a thousand miles or two.

Things had been smoothed as much as possible for him in the Tombs, for money and the power of it will go far toward ironing out even the corrugated routine of that big jail. He had a large cell to himself in the airiest, brightest corridor. His meals were served by a caterer from outside. Although he ate them without knife or fork, he soon learned that a spoon and the fingers can accomplish a good deal when backed by a good appetite, and Mr. Trimm's appetite was uniformly good. The warden and his underlings had been models of official kindliness; the newspapers had sent their brightest young men to interview him whenever he felt like talking, which wasn't often; and surely his lawyers had done all in his behalf that money —

a great deal of money — could do. Perhaps it was because of these things that Mr. Trimm had never been able to bring himself to realize that he was the Hobart W. Trimm who had been sentenced to the Federal prison; it seemed to him, somehow, that he, personally, was merely a spectator standing to one side watching the fight of another man to dodge the penitentiary.

However, he didn't fail to give the other man the advantage of every chance that money would buy. This sense of aloofness to the whole thing had persisted even when his personal lawyer came to him one night in the early fall and told him that the court of last possible resort had denied the last possible motion. Mr. Trimm cut the lawyer short with a shake of his head as the other began saying something about the chances of a pardon from the President. Mr. Trimm wasn't in the habit of letting men deceive him with idle words. No President would pardon him, and he knew it.

"Never mind that, Walling," he said steadily, when the lawyer offered to come to see him again before he started for prison the next day. "If you'll see that a drawing-room on the train is reserved for me — for us, I mean — and all that sort of thing, I'll not detain you any further. I have a good many things to do tonight. Good night."

"Such a man, such a man," said Walling to himself as he climbed into his car; "all chilled steel and brains. And they are going to lock that brain up for twelve years. It's a crime," said Walling, and shook his head. Walling always said it was a crime when they sent a client of his to prison. To his credit be it said, though, they sent very few of them there. Walling made as high as fifty thousand a year at criminal law. Some of it was very criminal law indeed. His specialty was picking holes in the statutes faster than the legislature could make them and provide them and putty them up with amendments. This was the first case he had lost in a good long time.

When Jerry, the turnkey, came for him in the morning Mr. Trimm had made as careful a toilet as the limited means at his command permitted, and he had eaten a hearty breakfast and was ready to go, all but putting on his hat. Looking the picture of well-groomed, close-buttoned, iron-gray middle age, Mr. Trimm followed the turnkey through the long corridor and down the winding iron stairs to the warden's office. He gave no heed to the curious eyes that followed him through the barred doors of many cells; his feet rang briskly on the flags.

The warden, Hallam, was there in the private office with another man, a tall, raw-boned man with a drooping, straw-colored mustache and the unmistakable look about him of the police officer. Mr. Trimm knew without being told that this was the man who would take him to prison. The stranger was standing at a desk, signing some papers.

"Sit down, please, Mr. Trimm," said the warden with a nervous cordiality. "Be through here in just one minute. This is Deputy Marshal Meyers," he added.

Mr. Trimm started to tell this Mr. Meyers he was glad to meet him, but caught himself and merely nodded. The man stared at him with neither interest nor curiosity in his dull blue eyes. The warden moved over toward the door.

"Mr. Trimm," he said, clearing his throat, "I took the liberty of calling a cab to take you gents up to the Grand Central. It's out front now. But there's a big crowd of reporters and photographers and a lot of other people waiting, and if I was you I'd slip out the back way — one of my men will open the yard gate for you — and jump aboard the subway down at Worth Street. Then you'll miss those fellows."

"Thank you, Warden — very kind of you," said Mr. Trimm in that crisp, businesslike way of his. He had been crisp and businesslike all his life. He heard a door opening softly behind him, and when he turned to look he saw the warden slipping out, furtively, in almost an embarrassed fashion.

"Well," said Meyers, "all ready?"

"Yes," said Mr. Trimm, and he made as if to rise.

"Wait one minute," said Meyers.

He half turned his back on Mr. Trimm and fumbled at the side pocket of his ill-hanging coat. Something inside of Mr. Trimm gave the least little jump, and the question that had ticked away so busily all those months began to buzz, buzz in his ears; but it was only a handkerchief the man was getting out. Doubtless he was going to mop his face.

He didn't mop his face, though. He unrolled the handkerchief slowly, as if it contained something immensely fragile and valuable, and then, thrusting it back in his pocket, he faced Mr. Trimm. He was carrying in his hands a pair of handcuffs that hung open-jawed. The jaws had little notches in them, like teeth that could bite. The question that had ticked in Mr. Trimm's head was answered at last — in the sight of these steel things with their notched jaws.

Mr. Trimm stood up and, with a movement as near to hesitation as he had ever been guilty of in his life, held out his hands, backs upward.

"I guess you're new at this kind of thing," said Meyers, grinning. "This here way — one at a time."

He took hold of Mr. Trimm's right hand, turned it sideways and settled one of the steel cuffs over the top of the wrist, flipping the notched jaw up from beneath and pressing it in so that it locked automatically with a brisk little click. Slipping the locked cuff back and forth on Mr. Trimm's lower arm like a man adjusting a part of machinery, and then bringing the left hand up to meet the right, he treated it the same way. Then he stepped back.

Mr. Trimm hadn't meant to protest. The word came unbidden.

"This — this isn't necessary, is it?" he asked in a voice that was husky and didn't seem to belong to him.

"Yep," said Meyers. "Standin' orders is play no favorites and take no chances. But you won't find them things uncomfortable. Lightest pair there was in the office, and I fixed 'em plenty loose."

For half a minute Mr. Trimm stood like a rooster hypnotized by a chalkmark, his arms extended, his eyes set on his bonds. His hands had fallen perhaps four inches apart, and in the space between his wrists a little chain was stretched taut. In the mounting tumult that filled his brain there sprang before Mr. Trimm's consciousness a phrase he had heard or read somewhere, the title of a story or, perhaps, it was a headline — The Grips of the Law. The Grips of the Law were upon Mr. Trimm — he felt them now for the first time in these shiny wristlets and this bit of chain that bound his wrists and filled his whole body with a strange, sinking feeling that made him physically sick. A sudden sweat beaded out on Mr. Trimm's face, turning it slick and wet.

He had a handkerchief, a fine linen handkerchief with a hemstitched border and a monogram on it, in the upper breast pocket of his buttoned coat. He tried to reach it. His hands went up, twisting awkwardly like crab claws. The fingers of both plucked out the handkerchief. Holding it so, Mr. Trimm mopped the sweat away. The links of the handcuffs fell in upon one another and lengthened out again at each movement, filling the room with a smart little sound.

He got the handkerchief stowed away with the same clumsiness. He raised the manacled hands to his hat brim, gave it a downward pull that brought it over his face and then, letting his short arms slide down upon his plump stomach, he faced the man who had put the fetters upon him, squaring his shoulders back. But it was hard, somehow, for him to square his shoulders — perhaps because of his hands being drawn so closely together. And his eyes would waver and fall upon his wrists. Mr. Trimm had a feeling that the skin must be stretched very tight on his jawbones and his forehead.

"Isn't there some way to hide these — these things?"

He began by blurting and ended by faltering it. His hands shuffled together, one over, then under the other.

"Here's a way," said Meyers. "This'll help."

He bestirred himself, folding one of the chained hands upon the other, tugging at the white linen cuffs and drawing the coat sleeves of his prisoner down over the bonds as far as the chain would let them come.

"There's the notion," he said. "Just do that-a-way and them bracelets won't hardly show a-tall. Ready? Let's be movin', then."

But handcuffs were never meant to be hidden. Merely a pair of steel rings clamped to one's wrists and coupled together with a scrap of chain, but they'll twist your arms and hamper the movements of your body in a way to constantly catch the eye of the passer-by. When a man is coming toward you, you can tell that he is handcuffed before you see the cuffs.

Mr. Trimm was never able to recall afterward exactly how he got out of the Tombs. He had a confused memory of a gate that was swung open by some one whom Mr. Trimm saw only from the feet to the waist; then he and his companion were out on Lafayette Street, speeding south toward the subway entrance at Worth Street, two blocks below, with the marshal's hand cupped under Mr. Trimm's right elbow and Mr. Trimm's plump legs almost trotting in their haste. For a moment it looked as if the warden's well-meant artifice would serve them.

But New York reporters are up to the tricks of people who want to evade them. At the sight of them a sentry reporter on the corner shouted a warning which was instantly caught up and passed on by another picket stationed half-way down the block; and around the wall of the Tombs came pelting a flying mob of newspaper photographers and reporters, with a choice rabble behind them. Foot passengers took up the chase, not knowing what it was about, but sensing a free show. Truckmen halted their teams, jumped down from their wagon seats and joined in. A man-chase is one of the pleasantest outdoor sports that a big city like New York can offer its people.

Fairly running now, the manacled banker and the deputy marshal shot down the winding steps into the subway a good ten yards ahead of the foremost pursuers. But there was one delay, while Meyers skirmished with his free hand in his trousers' pocket for a dime for the tickets, and another before a northbound local rolled into the station. Shouted at, jeered at, shoved this way and that, panting in gulping breaths, for he was stout by nature and staled by lack of exercise, Mr. Trimm, with Meyers clutching him by the arm, was fairly shot aboard one of the cars, at the apex of a human wedge. The astonished guard sensed the situation as the scrooging, shoving, noisy wave rolled across the platform toward the doors which he had opened and, thrusting the officer and his prisoner into the narrow platform space behind him, he tried to form with his body a barrier against those who came jamming in.

It didn't do any good. He was brushed away, protesting and blustering. The excitement spread through the train, and men, and even women, left their seats, overflowing the aisles.

There is no crueler thing than a city crowd, all eyes and morbid curiosity. But Mr. Trimm didn't see the staring eyes on that ride to the Grand Central. What he saw was many shifting feet and a hedge of legs shutting him in closely — those and the things on his wrists. What the eyes of the crowd saw was a small, stout man who, for all his bulk, seemed to have dried up inside his clothes so that they bagged on him some places and bulged others, with his head tucked on his chest, his hat over his face and his fingers straining to hold his coat sleeves down over a pair of steel bracelets.

Mr. Trimm gave mental thanks to a Deity whose existence he thought he had forgotten when the gate of the train-shed clanged behind him, shutting out the mob that had come with them all the way. Cameras had been shoved in his face like gun muzzles, reporters had scuttled alongside him, dodging under Meyers' fending arm to shout questions in his ears. He had neither spoken nor looked at them. The sweat still ran down his face, so that when finally he raised his head in the comparative quiet of the train-shed his skin was a curious gray under the jail paleness like the color of wet wood ashes.

"My lawyer promised to arrange for a compartment — for some private place on the train," he said to Meyers. "The conductor ought to know."

They were the first words he had uttered since he left the Tombs. Meyers spoke to a jaunty Pullman conductor who stood alongside the car where they had halted.

"No such reservation," said the conductor, running through his sheaf of slips, with his eyes shifting from Mr. Trimm's face to Mr. Trimm's hands and back again, as though he couldn't decide which was the more interesting part of him; "must be some mistake. Or else it was for some other train. Too late to change now — we pull out in three minutes."

"I reckon we better git on the smoker," said Meyers, "if there's room there."

Mr. Trimm was steered back again the length of the train through a double row of pop-eyed porters and staring trainmen. At the steps where they stopped the instinct to stretch out one hand and swing himself up by the rail operated automatically and his wrists got a nasty twist. Meyers and a brakeman practically lifted him up the steps and Meyers headed him into a car that was hazy with blue tobacco smoke. He was confused in his gait, almost as if his lower limbs had been fettered, too.

The car was full of shirt-sleeved men who stood up, craning their necks and stumbling over each other in their desire to see him. These men came out into the aisle, so that Meyers had to shove through them.

"This here'll do as well as any, I guess," said Meyers. He drew Mr. Trimm past him into the seat nearer the window and sat down alongside him on the side next the aisle, settling himself on the stuffy plush seat and breathing deeply, like a man who had got through the hardest part of a not easy job.

"Smoke?" he asked.

Mr. Trimm shook his head without raising it.

"Them cuffs feel plenty easy?" was the deputy's next question. He lifted Mr. Trimm's hands as casually as if they had been his hands and not Mr. Trimm's, and looked at them.

"Seem to be all right," he said as he let them fall back. "Don't pinch none, I reckon?" There was no answer.

The deputy tugged a minute at his mustache, searching his arid mind. An idea came to him. He drew a newspaper from his pocket, opened it out flat and spread it over Mr. Trimm's lap so that it covered the chained wrists. Almost instantly the train was in motion, moving through the yards.

"Be there in two hours more," volunteered Meyers. It was late afternoon. They were sliding through woodlands with occasional openings which showed meadows melting into wide, flat lands.

"Want a drink?" said the deputy, next. "No? Well, I guess I'll have a drop myself. Travelin' fills a feller's throat full of dust." He got up, lurching to the motion of the flying train, and started forward to the water cooler behind the car door. He had gone perhaps two-thirds of the way when Mr. Trimm felt a queer, grinding sensation beneath his feet; it was exactly as though the train were trying to go forward and back at the same time. Almost slowly, it seemed to him, the forward end of the car slued out of its straight course, at the same time tilting up. There was a grinding, roaring, grating sound, and before Mr. Trimm's eyes Meyers vanished, tumbling forward out of sight as the car floor buckled under his feet. Then, as everything — the train, the earth, the sky — all fused together in a great spatter of white and black, Mr. Trimm, plucked from his seat as though a giant hand had him by the collar, shot forward through the air over the seatbacks, his chained hands aloft, clutching wildly. He rolled out of a ragged opening where the smoker had broken in two, flopped gently on the sloping side of the right-of-way and slid easily to the bottom, where he lay quiet and still on his back in a bed of weeds and wild grass, staring straight up.

How many minutes he lay there Mr. Trimm didn't know. It may have been the shrieks of the victims or the glare from the fire that brought him out of the daze. He wriggled his body to a sitting posture, got on his feet, holding his head between his coupled hands, and gazed full-face into the crowning railroad horror of the year.

There were numbers of the passengers who had escaped serious hurt, but for the most part these persons seemed to have gone daft from terror and shock. Some were running aimlessly up and down and some, a few, were pecking feebly with improvised tools at the wreck, an indescribable jumble of ruin, from which there issued cries of mortal agony, and from which, at a point where two locomotives were lying on their sides, jammed together like fighting bucks that had died with locked horns, a tall flame already rippled and spread, sending up a pillar of black smoke that rose straight, poisoning the clear blue of the sky. Nobody paid any attention to Mr. Trimm as he stood swaying upon his feet. There wasn't a scratch on him. His clothes were hardly rumpled, his hat was still on his head. He stood a minute and then, moved by a sudden impulse, he turned round and went running straight away from the railroad at the best speed his pudgy legs could accomplish, with his arms pumping up and down in front of him and his fingers interlaced. It was a grotesque gait, almost like a rabbit hopping on its hindlegs.

Instantly, almost, the friendly woods growing down to the edge of the fill swallowed him up. He dodged and doubled back and forth among the tree trunks, his small, patent-leathered feet skipping nimbly over the irregular turf, until he stopped for lack of wind in his lungs to carry him another rod. When he had got his breath back Mr. Trimm leaned against a tree and bent his head this way and that, listening. No sound came to his ears except the sleepy calls of birds. As well as Mr. Trimm might judge he had come far into the depths of a considerable woodland. Already the shadows under the low limbs were growing thick and confused as the hurried twilight of early September came on.

Mr. Trimm sat down on a natural cushion of thick green moss between two roots of an oak. The place was clean and soft and sweet-scented. For some little time he sat there motionless, in a sort of mental haze. Then his round body slowly slid down flat upon the moss, his head lolled to one side and, the reaction having come, Mr. Trimm's limbs all relaxed and he went to sleep straightway.

After a while, when the woods were black and still, the half-grown moon came up and, sifting through a chink in the canopy of leaves above, shone down full on Mr. Trimm as he lay snoring gently with his mouth open, and his hands rising and falling on his breast. The moonlight struck upon the Little Giant handcuffs, making them look like quicksilver.

Toward daylight it turned off sharp and cool. The dogwoods which had been a solid color at nightfall now showed pink in one light and green in another, like changeable silk, as the first level rays of the sun came up over the rim of the earth and made long, golden lanes between the tree trunks. Mr. Trimm opened his eyes slowly, hardly sensing for the first moment or two how he came to be lying under a canopy of leaves, and gaped, seeking to stretch his arms. At that he remembered everything; he haunched his shoulders against the tree roots and wriggled himself up to a sitting position where he stayed for a while, letting his mind run over the sequence of events that had brought him where he was and taking inventory of the situation.

Of escape he had no thought. The hue and cry must be out for him before now; doubtless men were already searching for him. It would be better for him to walk in and surrender than to be taken in the woods like an animal escaped from a traveling menagerie. But the mere thought of enduring again what he had already gone through — the thought of being tagged by crowds and stared at, with his fetters on — filled him with a nausea. Nothing that the Federal penitentiary might hold in store for him could equal the black, blind shamefulness of yesterday; he knew that. The thought of the new ignominy that faced him made Mr. Trimm desperate. He had a desire to burrow into the thicket yonder and hide his face and his chained hands.

But perhaps he could get the handcuffs off and so go to meet his captors in some manner of dignity. Strange that the idea hadn't occurred to him before! It seemed to Mr. Trimm that he desired to get his two hands apart more than he had ever desired anything in his whole life before.

The hands had begun naturally to adjust themselves to their enforced companionship, and it wasn't such a very hard matter, though it cost him some painful wrenches and much twisting of the fingers, for Mr. Trimm to get his coat unbuttoned and his eyeglasses in their small leather case out of his upper waistcoat pocket. With the glasses on his nose he subjected his bonds to a critical examination. Each rounded steel band ran unbroken except for the smooth, almost jointless hinge and the small lock which sat perched on the back of the wrist in a little rounded excrescence like a steel wart. In the flat center of each lock was a small keyhole and alongside of it a notched nub, the nub being sunk in a minute depression. On the inner side, underneath, the cuffs slid into themselves — two notches on each showing where the jaws might be tightened to fit a smaller hand than his — and right over the large blue veins in the middle of the wrists were swivel links, shackle-bolted to the cuffs and connected by a flat, slightly larger middle link, giving the hands a palm-to-palm play of not more than four or five inches. The cuffs did not hurt — even after so many hours there was no actual discomfort from them and the flesh beneath them was hardly reddened.

But it didn't take Mr. Trimm long to find out that they were not to be got off. He tugged and pulled, trying with his fingers for a purchase. All he did was to chafe his skin and make his wrists throb with pain. The cuffs would go forward just so far, then the little humps of bone above the hands would catch and hold them.

Mr. Trimm was not a man to waste time in the pursuit of the obviously hopeless. Presently he stood up, shook himself and started off at a fair gait through the woods. The sun was up now and the turf was all dappled with lights and shadows, and about him much small, furtive wild life was stirring. He stepped along briskly, a strange figure for that green solitude, with his correct city garb and the glint of the steel at his sleeve ends.

Presently he heard the long-drawn, quavering, banshee wail of a locomotive. The sound came from almost behind him, in an opposite direction from where he supposed the track to be. So he turned around and went back the other way. He crossed a half-dried-up runlet and climbed a small hill, neither of which he remembered having met in his night from the wreck, and in a little while he came out upon the railroad. To the north a little distance the rails ran round a curve. To the south, where the diminishing rails running through the unbroken woodland met in a long, shiny V, he could see a big smoke smudge against the horizon. This smoke Mr. Trimm knew must come from the wreck — which was still burning, evidently. As nearly as he could judge he had come out of cover at least two miles above it. After a moment's consideration he decided to go south toward the wreck. Soon he could distinguish small dots like ants moving in and out about the black spot, and he knew these dots must be men.

A whining, whirring sound came along the rails to him from behind. He faced about just as a handcar shot out around the curve from the north, moving with amazing rapidity under the strokes of four men at the pumps. Other men, laborers to judge by their blue overalls, were sitting on the edges of the car with their feet dangling. For the second time within twelve hours impulse ruled Mr. Trimm, who wasn't given to impulses normally. He made a jump off the right-of-way, and as the handcar flashed by he watched its flight from the covert of a weed tangle.

But even as the handcar was passing him Mr. Trimm regretted his hastiness. He must surrender himself sooner or later; why not to these overalled laborers, since it was a thing that had to be done? He slid out of hiding and came trotting back to the tracks. Already the handcar was a hundred yards away, flitting into distance like some big, wonderfully fast bug, the figures of the men at the pumps rising and falling with a walking-beam regularity. As he stood watching them fade away and minded to try hailing them, yet still hesitating against his judgment, Mr. Trimm saw something white drop from the hands of one of the blue-clad figures on the handcar, unfold into a newspaper and come fluttering back along the tracks toward him. Just as he, starting doggedly ahead, met it, the little ground breeze that had carried it along died out and the paper dropped and flattened right in front of him. The front page was uppermost and he knew it must be of that morning's issue, for across the column tops ran the flaring headline: "Twenty Dead in Frightful Collision."

Squatting on the cindered track, Mr. Trimm patted the crumpled sheet flat with his hands. His eyes dropped from the first of the glaring captions to the second, to the next — and then his heart gave a great bound inside of him and, clutching up the newspaper to his breast, he bounded off the tracks back into another thicket and huddled there with the paper spread on the earth in front of him, reading by gulps while the chain that linked wrist to wrist tinkled to the tremors running through him. What he had seen first, in staring black-face type, was his own name leading the list of known dead, and what he saw now, broken up into choppy paragraphs and done in the nervous English of a trained reporter throwing a great news story together to catch an edition, but telling a clear enough story nevertheless, was a narrative in which his name recurred again and again. The body of the United States deputy marshal, Meyers, frightfully crushed, had been taken from the wreckage of the smoker — so the double-leaded story ran — and near to Meyers another body, with features burned beyond recognition, yet still retaining certain distinguishing marks of measurement and contour, had been found and identified as that of Hobart W. Trimm, the convicted banker. The bodies of these two, with eighteen other mangled dead, had been removed to a town called Westfield, from which town of Westfield the account of the disaster had been telegraphed to the New York paper. In another column farther along was more about Banker Trimm; facts about his soiled, selfish, greedy, successful life, his great fortune, his trial, and a statement that, lacking any close kin to claim his body, his lawyers had been notified.

Mr. Trimm read the account through to the end, and as he read the sense of dominant, masterful self-control came back to him in waves. He got up, taking the paper with him, and went back into the deeper woods, moving warily and watchfully. As he went his mind, trained to take hold of problems and wring the essence out of them, was busy. Of the charred, grisly thing in the improvised morgue at Westfield, wherever that might be, Mr. Trimm took no heed nor wasted any pity. All his life he had used live men to work his will, with no thought of what might come to them afterward. The living had served him, why not the dead?

He had other things to think of than this dead proxy of his. He was as good as free! There would be no hunt for him now; no alarm out, no posses combing every scrap of cover for a famous criminal turned fugitive. He had only to lie quiet a few days, somewhere, then get in secret touch with Walling. Walling would do anything for money. And he had the money — four millions and more, cannily saved from the crash that had ruined so many others.

He would alter his personal appearance, change his name — he thought of Duvall, which was his mother's name — and with Walling's aid he would get out of the country and into some other country where a man might live like a prince on four millions or the fractional part of it. He thought of South America, of South Africa, of a private yacht swinging through the little frequented islands of the South Seas. All that the law had tried to take from him would be given back. Walling would work out the details of the escape — and make it safe and sure — trust Walling for those things. On one side was the prison, with its promise of twelve grinding years sliced out of the very heart of his life; on the other, freedom, ease, security, even power. Through Mr. Trimm's mind tumbled thoughts of concessions, enterprises, privileges — the back corners of the globe were full of possibilities for the right man. And between this prospect and Mr. Trimm there stood nothing in the way, nothing but —

Mr. Trimm's eyes fell upon his bound hands. Snug-fitting, shiny steel bands irked his wrists. The Grips of the Law were still upon him.

But only in a way of speaking. It was preposterous, unbelievable, altogether out of the question that a man with four millions salted down and stored away, a man who all his life had been used to grappling with the big things and wrestling them down into submission, a man whose luck had come to be a byword — and had not it held good even in this last emergency? — would be balked by puny scraps of forged steel and a trumpery lock or two. Why, these cuffs were no thicker than the gold bands that Mr. Trimm had seen on the arms of overdressed women at the opera. The chain that joined them was no larger and, probably, no stronger than the chains which Mr. Trimm's chauffeur wrapped around the tires of the touring car in winter to keep the wheels from skidding on the slush. There would be a way, surely, for Mr. Trimm to free himself from these things. There must be — that was all there was to it.

Mr. Trimm looked himself over. His clothes were not badly rumpled; his patent-leather boots were scarcely scratched. Without the handcuffs he could pass unnoticed anywhere. By night then he must be free of them and on his way to some small inland city, to stay quiet there until the guarded telegram that he would send in cipher had reached Walling. There in the woods by himself Mr. Trimm no longer felt the ignominy of his bonds; he felt only the temporary embarrassment of them and the need of added precaution until he should have mastered them.

He was once more the unemotional man of affairs who had stood Wall Street on its esteemed head and caught the golden streams that trickled from its pockets. First making sure that he was in a well-screened covert of the woods he set about exploring all his pockets. The coat pockets were comparatively easy, now that he had got used to using two hands where one had always served, but it cost him a lot of twisting of his body and some pain to his mistreated wrist bones to bring forth the contents of his trousers' pockets. The chain kinked time and again as he groped with the undermost hand for the openings; his dumpy, pudgy form writhed grotesquely. But finally he finished. The search produced four cigars somewhat crumpled and frayed; some matches in a gun-metal case, a silver cigar cutter, two five-dollar bills, a handful of silver chicken feed, the leather case of the eyeglasses, a couple of quill toothpicks, a gold watch with a dangling fob, a notebook and some papers. Mr. Trimm ranged these things in a neat row upon a log, like a watchmaker setting out his kit, and took swift inventory of them. Some he eliminated from his design, stowing them back in the pockets easiest to reach. He kept for present employment the match safe, the cigar cutter and the watch.

This place where he had halted would suit his present purpose well, he decided. It was where an uprooted tree, fallen across an incurving bank, made a snug little recess that was closed in on three sides. Spreading the newspaper on the turf to save his knees from soiling, he knelt and set to his task. For the time he felt neither hunger nor thirst. He had found out during his earlier experiments that the nails of his little fingers, which were trimmed to a point, could invade the keyholes in the little steel warts on the backs of his wrists and touch the locks. The mechanism had even twitched a little bit under the tickle of the nail ends. So, having already smashed the gun-metal match safe under his heel, Mr. Trimm selected a slender-pointed bit from among its fragments and got to work, the left hand drawn up under the right, the fingers of the right busy with the lock of the left, the chain tightening and slackening with subdued clinking sounds at each movement.

Mr. Trimm didn't know much about picking a lock. He had got his money by a higher form of burglary that did not require a knowledge of lock picking. Nor as a boy had he been one to play at mechanics. He had let other boys make the toy fluttermills and the wooden traps and the like, and then he had traded for them. He was sorry now that he hadn't given more heed to the mechanical side of things when he was growing up.

He worked with a deliberate slowness, steadily. Nevertheless, it was hot work. The sun rose over the bank and shone on him through the limbs of the uprooted tree. His hat was on the ground alongside of him. The sweat ran down his face, streaking it and wilting his collar flat. The scrap of gun metal kept slipping out of his wet fingers. Down would go the chained hands to scrabble in the grass for it, and then the picking would go on again. This happened a good many times. Birds, nervous with the spirit that presages the fall migration, flew back and forth along the creek, almost grazing Mr. Trimm sometimes. A rain crow wove a brown thread in the green warp of the bushes above his head. A chattering red squirrel sat up on a tree limb to scold him. At intervals, distantly, came the cough of laboring trains, showing that the track must have been cleared. There were times when Mr. Trimm thought he felt the lock giving. These times he would work harder.

Late in the afternoon Mr. Trimm lay back against the bank, panting. His face was splotched with red, and the little hollows at the sides of his forehead pulsed rapidly up and down like the bellies of scared tree frogs. The bent outer case of the watch littered a bare patch on the log; its mainspring had gone the way of the fragments of the gun-metal match safe which were lying all about, each a worn-down, twisted wisp of metal. The spring of the eyeglasses had been confiscated long ago and the broken crystals powdered the earth where Mr. Trimm's toes had scraped a smooth patch. The nails of the two little fingers were worn to the quick and splintered down into the raw flesh. There were countless tiny scratches and mars on the locks of the handcuffs, and the steel wristbands were dulled with blood smears and pale-red tarnishes of new rust; but otherwise they were as stanch and strong a pair of Bean's Latest Model Little Giant handcuffs as you'd find in any hardware store anywhere.

The devilish, stupid malignity of the damned things! With an acid oath Mr. Trimm raised his hands and brought them down on the log violently. There was a double click and the bonds tightened painfully, pressing the chafed red skin white. Mr. Trimm snatched up his hands close to his near-sighted eyes and looked. One of the little notches on the under side of each cuff had disappeared. It was as if they were living things that had turned and bitten him for the blow he gave them.

From the time the sun went down there was a tingle of frost in the air. Mr. Trimm didn't sleep much. Under the squeeze of the tightened fetters his wrists throbbed steadily and racking cramps ran through his arms. His stomach felt as though it were tied into knots. The water that he drank from the branch only made his hunger sickness worse. His undergarments, that had been wet with perspiration, clung to him clammily. His middle-aged, tenderly-cared-for body called through every pore for clean linen and soap and water and rest, as his empty insides called for food.

After a while he became so chilled that the demand for warmth conquered his instinct for caution. He felt about him in the darkness, gathering scraps of dead wood, and, after breaking several of the matches that had been in the gun-metal match safe, he managed to strike one and with its tiny flame started a fire. He huddled almost over the fire, coughing when the smoke blew into his face and twisting and pulling at his arms in an effort to get relief from the everlasting cramps. It seemed to him that if he could only get an inch or two more of play for his hands he would be ever so much more comfortable. But he couldn't, of course.

He dozed, finally, sitting crosslegged with his head sunk between his hunched shoulders. A pain in a new place woke him. The fire had burned almost through the thin sole of his right shoe, and as he scrambled to his feet and stamped, the clap of the hot leather flat against his blistered foot almost made him cry out.

Soon after sunrise a boy came riding a horse down a faintly traced footpath along the creek, driving a cow with a bell on her neck ahead of him. Mr. Trimm's ears caught the sound of the clanking bell before either the cow or her herder was in sight, and he limped away, running, skulking through the thick cover. A pendent loop of a wild grapevine, swinging low, caught his hat and flipped it off his head; but Mr. Trimm, imagining pursuit, did not stop to pick it up and went on bareheaded until he had to stop from exhaustion. He saw some dark-red berries on a shrub upon which he had trod, and, stooping, he plucked some of them with his two hands and put three or four in his mouth experimentally. Warned instantly by the acrid, burning taste, he spat the crushed berries out and went on doggedly, following, according to his best judgment, a course parallel to the railroad. It was characteristic of him, a city-raised man, that he took no heed of distances nor of the distinguishing marks of the timber.

Behind a log at the edge of a small clearing in the woods he halted some little time, watching and listening. The clearing had grown up in sumacs and weeds and small saplings and it seemed deserted; certainly it was still. Near the center of it rose the sagging roof of what had been a shack or a shed of some sort. Stooping cautiously, to keep his bare head below the tops of the sumacs, Mr. Trimm made for the ruined shanty and gained it safely. In the midst of the rotted, punky logs that had once formed the walls he began scraping with his feet. Presently he uncovered something. It was a broken-off harrow tooth, scaled like a long, red fish with the crusted rust of years.

Mr. Trimm rested the lower rims of his handcuffs on the edge of an old, broken watering trough, worked the pointed end of the rust-crusted harrow tooth into the flat middle link of the chain as far as it would go, and then with one hand on top of the other he pressed downward with all his might. The pain in his wrists made him stop this at once. The link had not sprung or given in the least, but the twisting pressure had almost broken his wrist bones. He let the harrow tooth fall, knowing that it would never serve as a lever to free him — which, indeed, he had known all along — and sat on the side of the trough, rubbing his wrists and thinking.

He had another idea. It came into his mind as a vague suggestion that fire had certain effects upon certain metals. He kindled a fire of bits of the rotted wood, and when the flames ran together and rose slender and straight in a single red thread he thrust the chain into it, holding his hands as far apart as possible in the attitude of a player about to catch a bounced ball. But immediately the pain of that grew unendurable too, and he leaped back, jerking his hands away. He had succeeded only in blackening the steel and putting a big water blister on one of his wrists right where the shackle bolt would press upon it.

Where he huddled down in the shelter of one of the fallen walls he noticed, presently, a strand of rusted fence wire still held to half-tottering posts by a pair of blackened staples; it was part of a pen that had been used once for chickens or swine. Mr. Trimm tried the wire with his fingers. It was firm and springy. Rocking and groaning with the pain of it, he nevertheless began sliding the chain back and forth, back and forth along the strand of wire.

Eventually the wire, weakened by age, snapped in two. A tiny shined spot, hardly deep enough to be called a nick, in its tarnished, smudged surface was all the mark that the chain showed.

Staggering a little and putting his feet down unsteadily, Mr. Trimm left the clearing, heading as well as he could tell eastward, away from the railroad. After a mile or two he came to a dusty wood road winding downhill.

To the north of the clearing where Mr. Trimm had halted were a farm and a group of farm buildings. To the southward a mile or so was a cluster of dwellings set in the midst of more farm lands, with a shop or two and a small white church with a green spire in the center. Along a road that ran northward from the hamlet to the solitary farm a ten-year-old boy came, carrying a covered tin pail. A young gray squirrel flirted across the wagon ruts ahead of him and darted up a chestnut sapling. The boy put the pail down at the side of the road and began looking for a stone to throw at the squirrel.

Mr. Trimm slid out from behind a tree. A hemstitched handkerchief, grimed and stained, was loosely twisted around his wrists, partly hiding the handcuffs. He moved along with a queer, sliding gait, keeping as much of his body as he could turned from the youngster. The ears of the little chap caught the faint scuffle of feet and he spun around on his bare heel.

"My boy, would you —" Mr. Trimm began.

The boy's round eyes widened at the apparition that was sidling toward him in so strange a fashion, and then, taking fright, he dodged past Mr. Trimm and ran back the way he had come, as fast as his slim brown legs could take him. In half a minute he was out of sight round a bend.

Had the boy looked back he would have seen a still more curious spectacle than the one that had frightened him. He would have seen a man worth four million dollars down on his knees in the yellow dust, pawing with chained hands at the tight-fitting lid of the tin pail, and then, when he had got the lid off, drinking the fresh, warm milk which the pail held with great, choking gulps, uttering little mewing, animal sounds as he drank, while the white, creamy milk ran over his chin and splashed down his breast in little, spurting streams.

But the boy didn't look back. He ran all the way home and told his mother he had seen a wild man on the road to the village; and later, when his father came in from the fields, he was soundly thrashed for letting the sight of a tramp make him lose a good tin bucket and half a gallon of milk worth six cents a quart.

The rich, fresh milk put life into Mr. Trimm. He rested the better for it during the early part of that night in a haw thicket. Only the sharp, darting pains in his wrists kept rousing him to temporary wakefulness. In one of those intervals of waking the plan that had been sketchily forming in his mind from the time he had quit the clearing in the woods took on a definite, fixed shape. But how was he with safety to get the sort of aid he needed, and where?

Canvassing tentative plans in his head, he dozed off again.

On a smooth patch of turf behind the blacksmith shop three yokels were languidly pitching horseshoes — "quaits" they called them — at a stake driven in the earth. Just beyond, the woods shredded out into a long, yellow and green peninsula which stretched up almost to the back door of the smithy, so that late of afternoons the slanting shadows of the near-most trees fell on its roof of warped shingles. At the extreme end of this point of woods Mr. Trimm was squatted behind a big boulder, squinting warily through a thick-fringed curtain of ripened goldenrod tops and sumacs, heavy-headed with their dark-red tapers. He had been there more than an hour, cautiously waiting his chance to hail the blacksmith, whose figure he could make out in the smoky interior of his shop, passing back and forth in front of a smudgy forge fire and rattling metal against metal in intermittent fits of professional activity.

From where Mr. Trimm watched to where the horseshoe-pitching game went on was not more than sixty feet. He could hear what the players said and even see the little puffs of dust rise when one of them clapped his hands together after a pitch. He judged by the signs of slackening interest that they would be stopping soon and, he hoped, going clear away.

But the smith loafed out of his shop and, after an exchange of bucolic banter with the three of them, he took a hand in their game himself. He wore no coat or waistcoat and, as he poised a horseshoe for his first cast at the stake, Mr. Trimm saw, pinned flat against the broad strap of his suspenders, a shiny, silvery-looking disk. Having pitched the shoe, the smith moved over into the shade, so that he almost touched the clump of undergrowth that half buried Mr. Trimm's protecting boulder. The near-sighted eyes of the fugitive banker could make out then what the flat, silvery disk was, and Mr. Trimm cowered low in his covert behind the rock, holding his hands down between his knees, fearful that a gleam from his burnished wristlets might strike through the screen of weed growth and catch the inquiring eye of the smith. So he stayed, not daring to move, until a dinner horn sounded somewhere in the cluster of cottages beyond, and the smith, closing the doors of his shop, went away with the three yokels.

Then Mr. Trimm, stooping low, stole back into the deep woods again. In his extremity he was ready to risk making a bid for the hire of a blacksmith's aid to rid himself of his bonds, but not a blacksmith who wore a deputy sheriff's badge pinned to his suspenders.

He caught himself scraping his wrists up and down again against the rough, scrofulous trunk of a shellbark hickory. The irritation was comforting to the swollen skin. The cuffs, which kept catching on the bark and snagging small fragments of it loose, seemed to Mr. Trimm to have been a part and parcel of him for a long time — almost as long a time as he could remember. But the hands which they clasped so close seemed like the hands of somebody else. There was a numbness about them that made them feel as though they were a stranger's hands which never had belonged to him. As he looked at them with a sort of vague curiosity they seemed to swell and grow, these two strange, fettered hands, until they measured yards across, while the steel bands shrunk to the thinness of piano wire, cutting deeper and deeper into the flesh. Then the hands in turn began to shrink down and the cuffs to grow up into great, thick things as cumbersome as the couplings of a freight car. A voice that Mr. Trimm dimly recognized as his own was saying something about four million dollars over and over again.

Mr. Trimm roused up and shook his head angrily to clear it. He rubbed his eyes free of the clouding delusion. It wouldn't do for him to be getting light-headed.

On a flat, shelving bluff, forty feet above a cut through which the railroad ran at a point about five miles north of where the collision had occurred, a tramp was busy, just before sundown, cooking something in an old washboiler that perched precariously on a fire of wood coals. This tramp was tall and spindle-legged, with reddish hair and a pale, beardless, freckled face with no chin to it and not much forehead, so that it ran out to a peak like the profile of some featherless, unpleasant sort of fowl. The skirts of an old, ragged overcoat dangled grotesquely about his spare shanks.

Desperate as his plight had become, Mr. Trimm felt the old sick shame at the prospect of exposing himself to this knavish-looking vagabond whose help he meant to buy with a bribe. It was the sight of a dainty wisp of smoke from the wood fire curling upward through the cloudy, damp air that had brought him limping cautiously across the right-of-way, to climb the rocky shelf along the cut; but now he hesitated, shielded in the shadows twenty yards away. It was a whiff of something savory in the washboiler, borne to him on the still air and almost making him cry out with eagerness, that drew him forth finally. At the sound of the halting footsteps the tramp stopped stirring the mess in the washboiler and glanced up apprehensively. As he took in the figure of the newcomer his eyes narrowed and his pasty, nasty face spread in a grin of comprehension.

"Well, well, well," he said, leering offensively, "welcome to our city, little stranger."

Mr. Trimm came nearer, dragging his feet, for they were almost out of the wrecks of his patent-leather shoes. His gaze shifted from the tramp's face to the stuff on the fire, his nostrils wrinkling. Then slowly: "I'm in trouble," he said, and held out his hands.

"Wot I'd call a mild way o' puttin' it," said the tramp coolly. "That purticular kind o' joolry ain't gen'lly wore for pleasure."

His eyes took on a nervous squint and roved past Mr. Trimm's stooped figure down the slope of the hillock.

"Say, pal, how fur ahead are you of yore keeper?" he demanded, his manner changing.

"There is no one after me — no one that I know of," explained Mr. Trimm. "I am quite alone — I am certain of it."

"Sure there ain't nobody lookin' fur you?" the other persisted suspiciously.

"I tell you I am all alone," protested Mr. Trimm. "I want your help in getting these — these things off and sending a message to a friend. You'll be well paid, very well paid. I can pay you more money than you ever had in your life, probably, for your help. I can promise —"

He broke off, for the tramp, as if reassured by his words, had stooped again to his cooking and was stirring the bubbling contents of the washboiler with a peeled stick. The smell of the stew, rising strongly, filled Mr. Trimm with such a sharp and an aching hunger that he could not speak for a moment. He mastered himself, but the effort left him shaking and gulping.

"Go on, then, an' tell us somethin' about yourself," said the freckled man. "Wot brings you roamin' round this here railroad cut with them bracelets on?"

"I was in the wreck," obeyed Mr. Trimm. "The man with me — the officer — was killed. I wasn't hurt and I got away into these woods. But they think I'm dead too — my name was among the list of dead."

The other's peaky face lengthened in astonishment.

"Why, say," he began, "I read all about that there wreck — seen the list myself — say, you can't be Trimm, the New York banker? Yes, you are! Wot a streak of luck! Lemme look at you! Trimm, the swell financeer, sportin' 'round with the darbies on him all nice an' snug an' reg'lar! Mister Trimm — well, if this ain't rich!"

"My name is Trimm," said the starving banker miserably. "I've been wandering about here a great many hours — several days, I think it must be — and I need rest and food very much indeed. I don't — don't feel very well," he added, his voice trailing off.

At this his self-control gave way again and he began to quake violently as if with an ague. The smell of the cooking overcame him.

"You don't look so well an' that's a fact, Trimm," sneered the tramp, resuming his malicious, mocking air. "But set down an' make yourself at home, an' after a while, when this is done, we'll have a bite together — you an' me. It'll be a reg'lar tea party fur jest us two."

He broke off to chuckle. His mirth made him appear even more repulsive than before.

"But looky here, you wus sayin' somethin' about money," he said suddenly. "Le's take a look at all this here money."

He came over to him and went through Mr. Trimm's pockets. Mr. Trimm said nothing and stood quietly, making no resistance. The tramp finished a workmanlike search of the banker's pockets. He looked at the result as it lay in his grimy palm — a moist little wad of bills and some chicken-feed change — and spat disgustedly with a nasty oath.

"Well, Trimm," he said, "fur a Wall Street guy seems to me you travel purty light. About how much did you think you'd get done fur all this pile of wealth?"

"You will be well paid," said Mr. Trimm, arguing hard; "my friend will see to that. What I want you to do is to take the money you have there in your hand and buy a cold chisel or a file — any tools that will cut these things off me. And then you will send a telegram to a certain gentleman in New York. And let me stay with you until we get an answer — until he comes here. He will pay you well; I promise it."

He halted, his eyes and his mind again on the bubbling stuff in the rusted washboiler. The freckled vagrant studied him through his red-lidded eyes, kicking some loose embers back into the fire with his toe.

"I've heard a lot about you one way an' another, Trimm," he said. "'Tain't as if you wuz some pore down-an'-out devil tryin' to beat the cops out of doin' his bit in stir. You're the way-up, high-an'-mighty kind of crook. An' from wot I've read an' heard about you, you never toted fair with nobody yet. There wuz that young feller, wot's his name? — the cashier — him that wuz tried with you. He went along with you in yore games an' done yore

| 34 |

work fur you an' you let him go over the road to the same place you're tryin' to dodge now. Besides," he added cunningly, "you come here talkin' mighty big about money, yet I notice you ain't carryin' much of it in yore clothes. All I've had to go by is yore word. An' yore word ain't worth much, by all accounts."

"I tell you, man, that you'll profit richly," burst out Mr. Trimm, the words falling over each other in his new panic. "You must help me; I've endured too much — I've gone through too much to give up now." He pleaded fast, his hands shaking in a quiver of fear and eagerness as he stretched them out in entreaty and his linked chain shaking with them. Promises, pledges, commands, orders, arguments poured from him. His tormentor checked him with a gesture.

"You're wot I'd call a bird in the hand," he chuckled, hugging his slack frame, "an' it ain't fur you to be givin' orders — it's fur me. An', anyway, I guess we ain't a-goin' to be able to make a trade — leastwise not on yore terms. But we'll do business all right, all right — anyhow, I will."

"What do you mean?" panted Mr. Trimm, full of terror. "You'll help me?"

"I mean this," said the tramp slowly. He put his hands under his loose-hanging overcoat and began to fumble at a leather strap about his waist. "If I turn you over to the Government I know wot you'll be worth, purty near, by guessin' at the reward; an' besides, it'll maybe help to square me up fur one or two little matters. If I turn you loose I ain't got nothin' only your word — an' I've got an idea how much faith I kin put in that."

Mr. Trimm glanced about him wildly. There was no escape. He was fast in a trap which he himself had sprung. The thought of being led to jail, all foul of body and fettered as he was, by this filthy, smirking wretch made him crazy. He stumbled backward with some insane idea of running away.

"No hurry, no hurry a-tall," gloated the tramp, enjoying the torture of this helpless captive who had walked into his hands. "I ain't goin' to hurt you none — only make sure that you don't wander off an' hurt yourself while I'm gone. Won't do to let you be damagin' yoreself; you're valuable property. Trimm, now, I'll tell you wot we'll do! We'll just back you up agin one of these trees an' then we'll jest slip this here belt through yore elbows an' buckle it around behind at the back; an' I kinder guess you'll stay right there till I go down yonder to that station that I passed comin' up here an' see wot kind of a bargain I kin strike up with the marshal. Come on, now," he threatened with a show of bluster, reading the resolution that was mounting in Mr. Trimm's face. "Come on peaceable, if you don't want to git hurt."

Of a sudden Mr. Trimm became the primitive man. He was filled with those elemental emotions that make a man see in spatters of crimson. Gathering strength from passion out of an exhausted frame, he sprang forward at the tramp. He struck at him with his head, his shoulders, his knees, his manacled wrists, all at once. Not really hurt by the puny assault, but caught by surprise, the freckled man staggered back, clawing at the air, tripped on the washboiler in the fire, and with a yell vanished below the smooth edge of the cut.

Mr. Trimm stole forward and looked over the bluff. Half-way down the cliff on an outcropping shelf of rock the man lay, face downward, motionless. He seemed to have grown smaller and to have shrunk into his clothes. One long, thin leg was bent up under the skirts of the overcoat in a queer, twisted way, and the cloth of the trouser leg looked flattened and empty. As Mr. Trimm peered down at him he saw a red stain spreading on the rock under the still, silent figure's head.

Mr. Trimm turned to the washboiler. It lay on its side, empty, the last of its recent contents sputtering out into the half-drowned fire. He stared at this ruin a minute. Then without another look over the cliff edge he stumbled slowly down the hill, muttering to himself as he went. Just as he struck the level it began to rain, gently at first, then hard, and despite the shelter of the full-leaved forest trees, he was soon wet through to his skin and dripped water as he lurched along without sense of direction or, indeed, without any active realization of what he was doing.

Late that night it was still raining — a cold, steady, autumnal downpour. A huddled figure slowly climbed upon a low fence running about the house-yard of the little farm where the boy lived who got thrashed for losing a milkpail. On the wet top rail, precariously perching, the figure slipped and sprawled forward in the miry yard. It got up, painfully swaying on its feet. It was Mr. Trimm, looking for food. He moved slowly toward the house, tottering with weakness and because of the slick mud underfoot; peering near-sightedly this way and that through the murk; starting at every sound and stopping often to listen.

The outlines of a lean-to kitchen at the back of the house were looming dead ahead of him when from the corner of the cottage sprang a small terrier. It made for Mr. Trimm, barking shrilly. He retreated backward, kicking at the little dog and, to hold his balance, striking out with short, dabby jerks of his fettered hands — they were such motions as the terrier itself might make trying to walk on its hindlegs. Still backing away, expecting every instant to feel the terrier's teeth in his flesh, Mr. Trimm put one foot into a hotbed with a great clatter of the breaking glass. He felt the sharp ends of shattered glass tearing and cutting his shin as he jerked free. Recovering himself, he dealt the terrier a lucky kick under the throat that sent it back, yowling, to where it had come from, and then, as a door jerked open and a half-dressed man jumped out into the darkness, Mr. Trimm half hobbled, half fell out of sight behind the woodpile.

Back and forth along the lower edge of his yard the farmer hunted, with the whimpering, cowed terrier to guide him, poking in dark corners with the muzzle of his shotgun for the unseen intruder whose coming had aroused the household. In a brushpile just over the fence to the east Mr. Trimm lay on his face upon the wet earth, with the rain beating down on him, sobbing with choking gulps that wrenched him cruelly, biting at the bonds on his wrists until the sound of breaking teeth gritted in the air. Finally, in the hopeless, helpless frenzy of his agony he beat his arms up and down until the bracelets struck squarely on a flat stone and the force of the blow sent the cuffs home to the last notch so that they pressed harder and faster than ever upon the tortured wrist bones.

When he had wasted ten or fifteen minutes in a vain search the farmer went shivering back indoors to dry out his wet shirt. But the groveling figure in the brushpile lay for a long time where it was, only stirring a little while the rain dripped steadily down on everything.

––––––––––

The wreck was on a Tuesday evening. Early on the Saturday morning following the chief of police, who was likewise the whole of the day police force in the town of Westfield, nine miles from the place where the collision occurred, heard a peculiar, strangely weak knocking at the front door of his cottage, where he also had his office. The door was a Dutch door, sawed through the middle, so that the top half might be opened independently, leaving the lower panel fast. He swung this top half back.

A face was framed in the opening — an indescribably dirty, unutterably weary face, with matted white hair and a rime of whitish beard stubble on the jaws. It was fallen in and sunken and it drooped on the chest of its owner. The mouth, swollen and pulpy, as if from repeated hard blows, hung agape, and between the purplish parted lips showed the stumps of broken teeth. The eyes blinked weakly at the chief from under lids as colorless as the eyelids of a corpse. The bare white head was filthy with plastered mud and twigs, and dripping wet.

"Hello, there!" said the chief, startled at this apparition. "What do you want?"

With a movement that told of straining effort the lolled head came up off the chest. The thin, corded neck stiffened back, rising from a dirty, collarless neckband. The Adam's apple bulged out prominently, as big as a pigeon's egg.

"I have come," said the specter in a wheezing rasp of a voice which the chief could hardly hear — "I have come to surrender myself. I am Hobart W. Trimm."

"I guess you got another thing comin'," said the chief, who was by way of being a neighborhood wag. "When last seen Hobart W. Trimm was only fifty-two years old. Besides which, he's dead and buried. I guess maybe you'd better think agin, grandpap, and see if you ain't Methus'lah or the Wanderin' Jew."

"I am Hobart W. Trimm, the banker," whispered the stranger with a sort of wan stubbornness.

"Go on and prove it," suggested the chief, more than willing to prolong the enjoyment of the sensation. It wasn't often in Westfield that wandering lunatics came a-calling.

"Got any way to prove it?" he repeated as the visitor stared at him.

"Yes," came the creaking, rusted hinge of a voice, "I have."

Slowly, with struggling attempts, he raised his hands into the chief's sight. They were horribly swollen hands, red with the dried blood where they were not black with the dried dirt; the fingers puffed up out of shape; the nails broken; they were like the skinned paws of a bear. And at the wrists, almost buried in the bloated folds of flesh, blackened, rusted, battered, yet still strong and whole, was a tightly-locked pair of Bean's Latest Model Little Giant handcuffs.

"Great God!" cried the chief, transfixed at the sight. He drew the bolt and jerked open the lower half of the door.

"Come in," he said, "and lemme get them irons off of you — they must hurt something terrible."

"They can wait," said Mr. Trimm very feebly, very slowly and very humbly. "I have worn them a long, long while — I am used to them. Wouldn't you please get me some food first?"

II

THE BELLED BUZZARD

There was a swamp known as Little Niggerwool, to distinguish it from Big Niggerwool, which lay across the river. It was traversable only by those who knew it well — an oblong stretch of tawny mud and tawny water, measuring maybe four miles its longest way and two miles roughly at its widest; and it was full of cypress and stunted swamp oak, with edgings of canebrake and rank weeds; and in one place, where a ridge crossed it from side to side, it was snaggled like an old jaw with dead tree trunks, rising close-ranked and thick as teeth. It was untenanted of living things — except, down below, there were snakes and mosquitoes, and a few wading and swimming fowl; and up above, those big woodpeckers that the country people called logcocks — larger than pigeons, with flaming crests and spiky tails — swooping in their long, loping flight from snag to snag, always just out of gunshot of the chance invader, and uttering a strident cry which matched those surroundings so fitly that it might well have been the voice of the swamp itself.

On one side little Niggerwool drained its saffron waters off into a sluggish creek, where summer ducks bred, and on the other it ended abruptly at a natural bank of high ground, along which the county turnpike ran. The swamp came right up to the road and thrust its fringe of reedy, weedy undergrowth forward as though in challenge to the good farm lands that were spread beyond the barrier. At the time I am speaking of it was mid-summer, and from these canes and weeds and waterplants there came a smell so rank as almost to be overpowering. They grew thick as a curtain, making a blank green wall taller than a man's head.

Along the dusty stretch of road fronting the swamp nothing living had stirred for half an hour or more. And so at length the weed-stems rustled and parted, and out from among them a man came forth silently and cautiously. He was an old man — an old man who had once been fat, but with age had grown lean again, so that now his skin was by odds too large for him. It lay on the back of his neck in folds. Under the chin he was pouched like a pelican and about the jowls was wattled like a turkey gobbler.

He came out upon the road slowly and stopped there, switching his legs absently with the stalk of a horseweed. He was in his shirtsleeves — a respectable, snuffy old figure; evidently a man deliberate in words and thoughts and actions. There was something about him suggestive of an old staid sheep that had been engaged in a clandestine transaction and was afraid of being found out.

He had made amply sure no one was in sight before he came out of the swamp, but now, to be doubly certain, he watched the empty road — first up, then down — for a long half minute, and fetched a sighing breath of satisfaction. His eyes fell upon his feet, and, taken with an idea, he stepped back to the edge of the road and with a wisp of crabgrass wiped his shoes clean of the swamp mud, which was of a different color and texture from the soil of the upland. All his life Squire H. B. Gathers had been a careful, canny man, and he had need to be doubly careful on this summer morning. Having disposed of the mud on his feet, he settled his white straw hat down firmly upon his head, and, crossing the road, he climbed a stake-and-rider fence laboriously and went plodding sedately across a weedfield and up a slight slope toward his house, half a mile away, upon the crest of the little hill.

He felt perfectly natural — not like a man who had just taken a fellowman's life — but natural and safe, and well satisfied with himself and with his morning's work. And he was safe; that was the main thing — absolutely safe.

Without hitch or hindrance he had done the thing for which he had been planning and waiting and longing all these months. There had been no slip or mischance; the whole thing had worked out as plainly and simply as two and two make four. No living creature except himself knew of the meeting in the early morning at the head of Little Niggerwool, exactly where the squire had figured they should meet; none knew of the device by which the other man had been lured deeper and deeper in the swamp to the exact spot where the gun was hidden. No one had seen the two of them enter the swamp; no one had seen the squire emerge, three hours later, alone.

The gun, having served its purpose, was hidden again, in a place no mortal eye would ever discover. Face downward, with a hole between his shoulder blades, the dead man was lying where he might lie undiscovered for months or for years, or forever. His pedler's pack was buried in the mud so deep that not even the probing crawfishes could find it. He would never be missed probably. There was but the slightest likelihood that inquiry would ever be made for him — let alone a search. He was a stranger and a foreigner, the dead man was, whose comings and goings made no great stir in the neighborhood, and whose failure to come again would be taken as a matter of course — just one of those shiftless, wandering Dagoes, here today and gone tomorrow. That was one of the best things about it — these Dagoes never had any people in this country to worry about them or look for them when they disappeared. And so it was all over and done with, and nobody the wiser. The squire clapped his hands together briskly with the air of a man dismissing a subject from his mind for good, and mended his gait.

He felt no stabbings of conscience. On the contrary, a glow of gratification filled him. His house was saved from scandal; his present wife would philander no more — before his very eyes — with these young Dagoes, who came from nobody knew where, with packs on their backs and persuasive, wheedling tongues in their heads. At this thought the squire raised his head and considered his homestead. It looked good to him — the small white cottage among the honey locusts, with beehives and flower beds about it; the tidy whitewashed fence; the sound outbuildings at the back, and the well-tilled acres roundabout.

At the fence he halted and turned about, carelessly and casually, and looked back along the way he had come. Everything was as it should be — the weedfield steaming in the heat; the empty road stretching along the crooked ridge like a long gray snake sunning itself; and beyond it, massing up, the dark, cloaking stretch of swamp. Everything was all right, but — The squire's eyes, in their loose sacs of skin, narrowed and squinted. Out of the blue arch away over yonder a small black dot had resolved itself and was swinging to and fro, like a mote. A buzzard — hey? Well, there were always buzzards about on a clear day like this. Buzzards were nothing to worry about — almost any time you could see one buzzard, or a dozen buzzards if you were a mind to look for them.

But this particular buzzard now — wasn't he making for Little Niggerwool? The squire did not like the idea of that. He had not thought of the buzzards until this minute. Sometimes when cattle strayed the owners had been known to follow the buzzards, knowing mighty well that if the buzzards led the way to where the stray was, the stray would be past the small salvage of hide and hoofs — but the owner's doubts would be set at rest for good and all.

There was a grain of disquiet in this. The squire shook his head to drive the thought away — yet it persisted, coming back like a midge dancing before his face. Once at home, however, Squire Gathers deported himself in a perfectly normal manner. With the satisfied proprietorial eye of an elderly husband who has no rivals, he considered his young wife, busied about her household duties. He sat in an easy-chair upon his front gallery and read his yesterday's Courier-Journal which the rural carrier had brought him; but he kept stepping out into the yard to peer up into the sky and all about him. To the second Mrs. Gathers he explained that he was looking for weather signs. A day as hot and still as this one was a regular weather breeder; there ought to be rain before night.

"Maybe so," she said; "but looking's not going to bring rain."

Nevertheless the squire continued to look. There was really nothing to worry about; still at midday he did not eat much dinner, and before his wife was half through with hers he was back on the gallery. His paper was cast aside and he was watching. The original buzzard — or, anyhow, he judged it was the first one he had seen — was swinging back and forth in great pendulum swings, but closer down toward the swamp — closer and closer — until it looked from that distance as though the buzzard flew almost at the level of the tallest snags there. And on beyond this first buzzard, coursing above him, were other buzzards. Were there four of them? No; there were five — five in all.

Such is the way of the buzzard — that shifting black question mark which punctuates a Southern sky. In the woods a shoat or a sheep or a horse lies down to die. At once, coming seemingly out of nowhere, appears a black spot, up five hundred feet or a thousand in the air. In broad loops and swirls this dot swings round and round and round, coming a little closer to earth at every turn and always with one particular spot upon the earth for the axis of its wheel. Out of space also other moving spots emerge and grow larger as they tack and jib and drop nearer, coming in their leisurely buzzard way to the feast. There is no haste — the feast will wait. If it is a dumb creature that has fallen stricken the grim coursers will sooner or later be assembled about it and alongside it, scrouging ever closer and closer to the dying thing, with awkward out-thrustings of their naked necks and great dust-raising flaps of the huge, unkempt wings; lifting their feathered shanks high and stiffly like old crippled grave-diggers in overalls that are too tight — but silent and patient all, offering no attack until the last tremor runs through the stiffening carcass and the eyes glaze over. To humans the buzzard pays a deeper meed of respect — he hangs aloft longer; but in the end he comes. No scavenger shark, no carrion crab, ever chambered more grisly secrets in his digestive processes than this big charnel bird. Such is the way of the buzzard.

The squire missed his afternoon nap, a thing that had not happened in years. He stayed on the front gallery and kept count. Those moving distant black specks typified uneasiness for the squire — not fear exactly, or panic or anything akin to it, but a nibbling, nagging kind of uneasiness. Time and again he said to himself that he would not think about them any more; but he did — unceasingly.

By supper time there were seven of them.

He slept light and slept badly. It was not the thought of that dead man lying yonder in Little Niggerwool that made him toss and fume while his wife snored gently alongside him. It was something else altogether. Finally his stirrings roused her and she asked him drowsily what ailed him. Was he sick? Or bothered about anything?

Irritated, he answered her snappishly. Certainly nothing was bothering him, he told her. It was a hot enough night — wasn't it? And when a man got a little along in life he was apt to be a light sleeper — wasn't that so? Well, then? She turned upon her side and slept again with her light, purring snore. The squire lay awake, thinking hard and waiting for day to come.

At the first faint pink-and-gray glow he was up and out upon the gallery. He cut a comic figure standing there in his shirt in the half light, with the dewlap at his throat dangling grotesquely in the neck opening of the unbuttoned garment, and his bare bowed legs showing, splotched and varicose. He kept his eyes fixed on the skyline below, to the south. Buzzards are early risers too. Presently, as the heavens shimmered with the miracle of sunrise, he could make them out — six or seven, or maybe eight.

An hour after breakfast the squire was on his way down through the weedfield to the county road. He went half eagerly, half unwillingly. He wanted to make sure about those buzzards. It might be that they were aiming for the old pasture at the head of the swamp. There were sheep grazing there — and it might be that a sheep had died. Buzzards were notoriously fond of sheep, when dead. Or, if they were pointed for the swamp, he must satisfy himself exactly what part of the swamp it was. He was at the stake-and-rider fence when a mare came jogging down the road, drawing a rig with a man in it. At sight of the squire in the field the man pulled up.

"Hi, squire!" he saluted. "Goin' somewheres?"

"No; jest knockin' about," the squire said — "jest sorter lookin' the place over."

"Hot agin — ain't it?" said the other.

The squire allowed that it was, for a fact, mighty hot. Commonplaces of gossip followed this — county politics and a neighbor's wife sick of breakbone fever down the road a piece. The subject of crops succeeded inevitably. The squire spoke of the need of rain. Instantly he regretted it, for the other man, who was by way of being a weather wiseacre, cocked his head aloft to study the sky for any signs of clouds.

"Wonder whut all them buzzards are doin' yonder, squire," he said, pointing upward with his whipstock.

"Whut buzzards — where?" asked the squire with an elaborate note of carelessness in his voice.

"Right yonder, over Little Niggerwool — see 'em there?"

"Oh, yes," the squire made answer. "Now I see 'em. They ain't doin' nothin', I reckin — jest flyin' round same as they always do in clear weather."

"Must be somethin' dead over there!" speculated the man in the buggy.

"A hawg probably," said the squire promptly — almost too promptly. "There's likely to be hawgs usin' in Niggerwool. Bristow, over on the other side from here — he's got a big drove of hawgs."

"Well, mebbe so," said the man; "but hawgs is a heap more apt to be feedin' on high ground, seems like to me. Well, I'll be gittin' along towards town. G'day, squire." And he slapped the lines down on the mare's flank and jogged off through the dust.

He could not have suspected anything — that man couldn't. As the squire turned away from the road and headed for his house he congratulated himself upon that stroke of his in bringing in Bristow's hogs; and yet there remained this disquieting note in the situation, that buzzards flying, and especially buzzards flying over Little Niggerwool, made people curious — made them ask questions.

He was half-way across the weedfield when, above the hum of insect life, above the inward clamor of his own busy speculations, there came to his ear dimly and distantly a sound that made him halt and cant his head to one side the better to hear it. Somewhere, a good way off, there was a thin, thready, broken strain of metallic clinking and clanking — an eery ghost-chime ringing. It came nearer and became plainer — tonk-tonk-tonk; then the tonks all running together briskly.

A sheep bell or a cowbell — that was it; but why did it seem to come from overhead, from up in the sky, like? And why did it shift so abruptly from one quarter to another — from left to right and back again to left? And how was it that the clapper seemed to strike so fast? Not even the breachiest of breachy young heifers could be expected to tinkle a cowbell with such briskness. The squire's eye searched the earth and the sky, his troubled mind giving to his eye a quick and flashing scrutiny. He had it. It was not a cow at all. It was not anything that went on four legs.

One of the loathly flock had left the others. The orbit of his swing had carried him across the road and over Squire Gathers' land. He was sailing right toward and over the squire now. Craning his flabby neck, the squire could make out the unwholesome contour of the huge bird. He could see the ragged black wings — a buzzard's wings are so often ragged and uneven — and the naked throat; the slim, naked head; the big feet folded up against the dingy belly. And he could see a bell too — an undersized cowbell — that dangled at the creature's breast and jangled incessantly. All his life nearly Squire Gathers had been hearing about the Belled Buzzard. Now with his own eye he was seeing him.

Once, years and years and years ago, some one trapped a buzzard, and before freeing it clamped about its skinny neck a copper band with a cowbell pendent from it. Since then the bird so ornamented has been seen a hundred times — and heard oftener — over an area as wide as half the continent. It has been reported, now in Kentucky, now in Texas, now in North Carolina — now anywhere between the Ohio River and the Gulf. Crossroads correspondents take their pens in hand to write to the country papers that on such and such a date, at such a place, So-and-So saw the Belled Buzzard. Always it is the Belled Buzzard, never a belled buzzard. The Belled Buzzard is an institution.

There must be more than one of them. It seems hard to believe that one bird, even a buzzard in his prime, and protected by law in every Southern state and known to be a bird of great age, could live so long and range so far and wear a clinking cowbell all the time! Probably other jokers have emulated the original joker; probably if the truth were known there have been a dozen such; but the country people will have it that there is only one Belled Buzzard — a bird that bears a charmed life and on his neck a never silent bell.

Squire Gathers regarded it a most untoward thing that the Belled Buzzard should have come just at this time. The movements of ordinary, unmarked buzzards mainly concerned only those whose stock had strayed; but almost anybody with time to spare might follow this rare and famous visitor, this belled and feathered junkman of the sky. Supposing now that some one followed it today — maybe followed it even to a certain thick clump of cypress in the middle of Little Niggerwool!

But at this particular moment the Belled Buzzard was heading directly away from that quarter. Could it be following him? Of course not! It was just by chance that it flew along the course the squire was taking. But, to make sure, he veered off sharply, away from the footpath into the high weeds so that the startled grasshoppers sprayed up in front of him in fan-like flights.

He was right; it was only a chance. The Belled Buzzard swung off too, but in the opposite direction, with a sharp tonking of its bell, and, flapping hard, was in a minute or two out of hearing and sight, past the trees to the westward.

Again the squire skimped his dinner, and again he spent the long drowsy afternoon upon his front gallery. In all the sky there were now no buzzards visible, belled or unbelled — they had settled to earth somewhere; and this served somewhat to soothe the squire's pestered mind. This does not mean, though, that he was by any means easy in his thoughts. Outwardly he was calm enough, with the ruminative judicial air befitting the oldest justice of the peace in the county; but, within him, a little something gnawed unceasingly at his nerves like one of those small white worms that are to be found in seemingly sound nuts. About once in so long a tiny spasm of the muscles would contract the dewlap under his chin. The squire had never heard of that play, made famous by a famous player, wherein the murdered victim was a pedler too, and a clamoring bell the voice of unappeasable remorse in the murderer's ear. As a strict churchgoer the squire had no use for players or for play actors, and so was spared that added canker to his conscience. It was bad enough as it was.

That night, as on the night before, the old man's sleep was broken and fitful and disturbed by dreaming, in which he heard a metal clapper striking against a brazen surface. This was one dream that came true. Just after daybreak he heaved himself out of bed, with a flop of his broad bare feet upon the floor, and stepped to the window and peered out. Half seen in the pinkish light, the Belled Buzzard flapped directly over his roof and flew due south, right toward the swamp — drawing a direct line through the air between the slayer and the victim — or, anyway, so it seemed to the watcher, grown suddenly tremulous.

Knee deep in yellow swamp water the squire squatted, with his shotgun cocked and loaded and ready, waiting to kill the bird that now typified for him guilt and danger and an abiding great fear. Gnats plagued him and about him frogs croaked. Almost overhead a log-cock clung lengthwise to a snag, watching him. Snake doctors, limber, long insects with bronze bodies and filmy wings, went back and forth like small living shuttles. Other buzzards passed and repassed, but the squire waited, forgetting the cramps in his elderly limbs and the discomfort of the water in his shoes.

At length he heard the bell. It came nearer and nearer, and the Belled Buzzard swung overhead not sixty feet up, its black bulk a fair target against the blue. He aimed and fired, both barrels bellowing at once and a fog of thick powder smoke enveloping him. Through the smoke he saw the bird career and its bell jangled furiously; then the buzzard righted itself and was gone, fleeing so fast that the sound of its bell was hushed almost instantly. Two long wing feathers drifted slowly down; torn disks of gunwadding and shredded green scraps of leaves descended about the squire in a little shower.

He cast his empty gun from him so that it fell in the water and disappeared; and he hurried out of the swamp as fast as his shaky legs would take him, splashing himself with mire and water to his eyebrows. Mucked with mud, breathing in great gulps, trembling, a suspicious figure to any eye, he burst through the weed curtain and staggered into the open, his caution all gone and a vast desperation fairly choking him — but the gray road was empty and the field beyond the road was empty; and, except for him, the whole world seemed empty and silent.

As he crossed the field Squire Gathers composed himself. With plucked handfuls of grass he cleansed himself of much of the swamp mire that coated him over; but the little white worm that gnawed at his nerves had become a cold snake that was coiled about his heart, squeezing it tighter and tighter!

This episode of the attempt to kill the Belled Buzzard occurred in the afternoon of the third day. In the forenoon of the fourth, the weather being still hot, with cloudless skies and no air stirring, there was a rattle of warped wheels in the squire's lane and a hail at his yard fence. Coming out upon his gallery from the innermost darkened room of his house, where he had been stretched upon a bed, the squire shaded his eyes from the glare and saw the constable of his own magisterial district sitting in a buggy at the gate waiting.

The old man went down the dirtpath slowly, almost reluctantly, with his head twisted up side wise, listening, watching; but the constable sensed nothing strange about the other's gait and posture; the constable was full of the news he brought. He began to unload the burden of it without preamble.

"Mornin', Squire Gathers. There's been a dead man found in Little Niggerwool — and you're wanted."

He did not notice that the squire was holding on with both hands to the gate; but he did notice that the squire had a sick look out of his eyes and a dead, pasty color in his face; and he noticed — but attached no meaning to it — that when the squire spoke his voice seemed flat and hollow.

"Wanted — fur — whut?" The squire forced the words out of his throat, pumped them out fairly.

"Why, to hold the inquest," explained the constable. "The coroner's sick abed, and he said you bein' the nearest jestice of the peace you should serve."

"Oh," said the squire with more ease. "Well, where is it — the body?"

"They taken it to Bristow's place and put it in his stable for the present. They brought it out over on that side and his place was the nearest. If you'll hop in here with me, squire, I'll ride you right over there now. There's enough men already gathered to make up a jury, I reckin."

"I — I ain't well," demurred the squire. "I've been sleepin' porely these last few nights. It's the heat," he added quickly.

"Well, suh, you don't look very brash, and that's a fact," said the constable; "but this here job ain't goin' to keep you long. You see it's in such shape — the body is — that there ain't no way of makin' out who the feller was nor whut killed him. There ain't nobody reported missin' in this county as we know of, either; so I jedge a verdict of a unknown person dead from unknown causes would be about the correct thing. And we kin git it all over mighty quick and put him underground right away, suh — if you'll go along now."

"I'll go," agreed the squire, almost quivering in his newborn eagerness. "I'll go right now." He did not wait to get his coat or to notify his wife of the errand that was taking him. In his shirtsleeves he climbed into the buggy, and the constable turned his horse and clucked him into a trot. And now the squire asked the question that knocked at his lips demanding to be asked — the question the answer to which he yearned for and yet dreaded.

"How did they come to find — it?"

"Well, suh, that's a funny thing," said the constable. "Early this mornin' Bristow's oldest boy — that one they call Buddy — he heared a cowbell over in the swamp and so he went to look; Bristow's got cows, as you know, and one or two of 'em is belled. And he kept on followin' after the sound of it till he got way down into the thickest part of them cypress slashes that's near the middle there; and right there he run acrost it — this body.

"But, suh, squire, it wasn't no cow at all. No, suh; it was a buzzard with a cowbell on his neck — that's whut it was. Yes, suh; that there same old Belled Buzzard he's come back agin and is hangin' round. They tell me he ain't been seen round here since the year of the yellow fever — I don't remember myself, but that's whut they tell me. The niggers over on the other side are right smartly worked up over it. They say — the niggers do — that when the Belled

Buzzard comes it's a sign of bad luck for somebody, shore!"

The constable drove on, talking on, garrulous as a guinea hen. The squire didn't heed him. Hunched back in the buggy, he harkened only to those busy inner voices filling his mind with thundering portents. Even so, his ear was first to catch above the rattle of the buggy wheels the far-away, faint tonk-tonk! They were about half-way to Bristow's place then. He gave no sign, and it was perhaps half a minute before his companion heard it too.

The constable jerked the horse to a standstill and craned his neck over his shoulder.

"Well, by doctors!" he cried, "if there ain't the old scoundrel now, right here behind us! I kin see him plain as day — he's got an old cowbell hitched to his neck; and he's shy a couple of feathers out of one wing. By doctors, that's somethin' you won't see every day! In all my born days I ain't never seen the beat of that!"

Squire Gathers did not look; he only cowered back farther under the buggy top. In the pleasing excitement of the moment his companion took no heed, though, of anything except the Belled Buzzard.

"Is he followin' us?" asked the squire in a curiously flat, weighted voice.

"Which — him?" answered the constable, still stretching his neck. "No, he's gone now — gone off to the left — jest a-zoomin', like he'd done forgot somethin'."

And Bristow's place was to the left! But there might still be time. To get the inquest over and the body underground — those were the main things. Ordinarily humane in his treatment of stock, Squire Gathers urged the constable to greater speed. The horse was lathered and his sides heaved wearily as they pounded across the bridge over the creek which was the outlet to the swamp and emerged from a patch of woods in sight of Bristow's farm buildings.

The house was set on a little hill among cleared fields and was in other respects much like the squire's own house except that it was smaller and not so well painted. There was a wide yard in front with shade trees and a lye hopper and a well-box, and a paling fence with a stile in it instead of a gate. At the rear, behind a clutter of outbuildings — a barn, a smokehouse and a corncrib — was a little peach orchard, and flanking the house on the right there was a good-sized cowyard, empty of stock at this hour, with feedracks ranged in a row against the fence. A two-year-old negro child, bareheaded and barefooted and wearing but a single garment, was grubbing busily in the dirt under one of these feedracks.

To the front fence a dozen or more riding horses were hitched, flicking their tails at the flies; and on the gallery men in their shirtsleeves were grouped. An old negro woman, with her head tied in a bandanna and a man's old slouch hat perched upon the bandanna, peeped out from behind a corner. There were gaunt hound dogs wandering about, sniffing uneasily.

Before the constable had the horse hitched the squire was out of the buggy and on his way up the footpath, going at a brisker step than the squire usually traveled. The men on the porch hailed him gravely and ceremoniously, as befitting an occasion of solemnity. Afterward some of them recalled the look in his eye; but at the moment they noted it — if they noted it at all — subconsciously.

For all his haste the squire, as was also remembered later, was almost the last to enter the door; and before he did enter he halted and searched the flawless sky as though for signs of rain. Then he hurried on after the others, who clumped single file along a narrow little hall, the bare, uncarpeted floor creaking loudly under their heavy farm shoes, and entered a good-sized room that had in it, among other things, a high-piled feather bed and a cottage organ — Bristow's best room, now to be placed at the disposal of the law's representatives for the inquest. The squire took the largest chair and drew it to the very center of the room, in front of a fireplace, where the grate was banked with withering asparagus ferns. The constable took his place formally at one side of the presiding official. The others sat or stood about where they could find room — all but six of them, whom the squire picked for his coroner's jury, and who backed themselves against the wall.

The squire showed haste. He drove the preliminaries forward with a sort of tremulous insistence. Bristow's wife brought a bucket of fresh drinking water and a gourd, and almost before she was out of the room and the door closed behind her the squire had sworn his jurors and was calling the first witness, who it seemed likely would also be the only witness — Bristow's oldest boy. The boy wriggled in confusion as he sat on a cane-bottomed chair facing the old magistrate. All there, barring one or two, had heard his story a dozen times already, but now it was to be repeated under oath; and so they bent their heads, listening as though it were a brand-new tale. All eyes were on him; none were fastened on the squire as he, too, gravely bent his head, listening — listening.

The witness began — but had no more than started when the squire gave a great, screeching howl and sprang from his chair and staggered backward, his eyes popped and the pouch under his chin quivering as though it had a separate life all its own. Startled, the constable made toward him and they struck together heavily and went down — both on their all fours — right in front of the fireplace.

The constable scrambled free and got upon his feet, in a squat of astonishment, with his head craned; but the squire stayed upon the floor, face downward, his feet flopping among the rustling asparagus greens — a picture of slavering animal fear. And now his gagging screech resolved itself into articulate speech.

"I done it!" they made out his shrieked words. "I done it! I own up — I killed him! He aimed fur to break up my home and I tolled him off into Niggerwool and killed him! There's a hole in his back if you'll look fur it. I done it — oh, I done it — and I'll tell everything jest like it happened if you'll jest keep that thing away from me! Oh, my Lawdy! Don't you hear it? It's a-comin' clos'ter and clos'ter — it's a-comin' after me! Keep it away —" His voice gave out and he buried his head in his hands and rolled upon the gaudy carpet.

And now they all heard what he had heard first — they heard the tonk-tonk-tonk of a cowbell, coming near and nearer toward them along the hallway without. It was as though the sound floated along. There was no creak of footsteps upon the loose, bare boards — and the bell jangled faster than it would dangling from a cow's neck. The sound came right to the door and Squire Gathers wallowed among the chair legs.

The door swung open. In the doorway stood a negro child, barefooted and naked except for a single garment, eyeing them with serious, rolling eyes — and, with all the strength of his two puny arms, proudly but solemnly tolling a small rusty cowbell he had found in the cowyard.

III

AN OCCURRENCE UP A
SIDE STREET

"See if he's still there, will you?" said the man listlessly, as if knowing in advance what the answer would be.

The woman, who, like the man, was in her stocking feet, crossed the room, closing the door with all softness behind her. She felt her way silently through the darkness of a small hallway, putting first her ear and then her eye to a tiny cranny in some thick curtains at a front window.

She looked downward and outward upon one of those New York side streets that is precisely like forty other New York side streets: two unbroken lines of high-shouldered, narrow-chested brick-and-stone houses, rising in abrupt, straight cliffs; at the bottom of the canyon a narrow river of roadway with manholes and conduit covers dotting its channel intermittently like scattered stepping stones; and on either side wide, flat pavements, as though the stream had fallen to low-water mark and left bare its shallow banks. Daylight would have shown most of the houses boarded up, with diamond-shaped vents, like leering eyes, cut in the painted planking of the windows and doors; but now it was night time — eleven o'clock of a wet, hot, humid night of the late summer — and the street was buttoned down its length in the double-breasted fashion of a bandmaster's coat with twin rows of gas lamps evenly spaced. Under each small circle of lighted space the dripping, black asphalt had a slimy, slick look like the sides of a newly caught catfish. Elsewhere the whole vista lay all in close shadow, black as a cave mouth under every stoop front and blacker still in the hooded basement areas. Only, half a mile to the eastward a dim, distant flicker showed where Broadway ran, a broad, yellow streak down the spine of the city, and high above the broken skyline of eaves and cornices there rolled in cloudy waves the sullen red radiance, born of a million electrics and the flares from gas tanks and chimneys, which is only to be seen on such nights as this, giving to the heaven above New York that same color tone you find in an artist's conception of Babylon falling or Rome burning.

From where the woman stood at the window she could make out the round, white, mushroom top of a policeman's summer helmet as its wearer leaned back, half sheltered under the narrow portico of the stoop just below her; and she could see his uniform sleeve and his hand, covered with a white cotton glove, come up, carrying a handkerchief, and mop the hidden face under the helmet's brim. The squeak of his heavy shoes was plainly audible to her also. While she stayed there, watching and listening, two pedestrians — and only two — passed on her side of the street: a messenger boy in a glistening rubber poncho going west and a man under an umbrella going east. Each was hurrying along until he came just opposite her, and then, as though controlled by the same set of strings, each stopped short and looked up curiously at the blind, dark house and at the figure lounging in the doorway, then hurried on without a word, leaving the silent policeman fretfully mopping his moist face and tugging at the wilted collar about his neck.

After a minute or two at her peephole behind the window curtains above, the woman passed back through the door to the inner, middle room where the man sat.

"Still there," she said lifelessly in the half whisper that she had come to use almost altogether these last few days; "still there and sure to stay there until another one just like him comes to take his place. What else did you expect?"

The man only nodded absently and went on peeling an overripe peach, striking out constantly, with the hand that held the knife, at the flies. They were green flies — huge, shiny-backed, buzzing, persistent vermin. There were a thousand of them; there seemed to be a million of them. They filled the shut-in room with their vile humming; they swarmed everywhere in the half light. They were thickest, though, in a corner at the back, where there was a closed, white door. Here a great knot of them, like an iridescent, shimmering jewel, was clustered about the keyhole. They scrolled the white enameled panels with intricate, shifting patterns, and in pairs and singly they promenaded busily on the white porcelain knob, giving it the appearance of being alive and having a motion of its own.

It was stiflingly hot and sticky in the room. The sweat rolled down the man's face as he peeled his peach and pared some half-rotted spots out of it. He protected it with a cupped palm as he bit into it. One huge green fly flipped nimbly under the fending hand and lit on the peach. With a savage little snarl of disgust and loathing the man shook the clinging insect off and with the knife carved away the place where its feet had touched the soft fruit. Then he went on munching, meanwhile furtively watching the woman. She was on the opposite side of a small center-table from him, with her face in her hands, shaking her head with a little shuddering motion whenever one of the flies settled on her close-cropped hair or brushed her bare neck.

He was a smallish man, with a suggestion of something dapper about him even in his present unkempt disorder; he might have been handsome, in a weakly effeminate way, had not Nature or some mishap given his face a twist that skewed it all to one side, drawing all of his features out of focus, like a reflection viewed in a flawed mirror. He was no heavier than the woman and hardly as tall. She, however, looked less than her real height, seeing that she was dressed, like a half-grown boy, in a soft-collared shirt open at the throat and a pair of loose trousers. She had large but rather regular features, pouting lips, a clear brown skin and full, prominent brown eyes; and one of them had a pronounced cast in it — an imperfection already made familiar by picture and printed description to sundry millions of newspaper readers. For this was Ella Gilmorris, the woman in the case of the Gilmorris murder, about which the continent of North America was now reading and talking. And the little man with the twisted face, who sat across from her, gnawing a peach stone clean, was the notorious "Doctor" Harris Devine, alias Vanderburg, her accomplice, and worth more now to society in his present untidy state than ever before at any one moment of his whole discreditable life, since for his capture the people of the state of New York stood willing to pay the sum of one thousand dollars, which tidy reward one of the afternoon papers had increased by another thousand.

Everywhere detectives — amateurs and the kind who work for hire — were seeking the pair who at this precise moment faced each other across a little center-table in the last place any searcher would have suspected or expected them to be — on the second floor of the house in which the late Cassius Gilmorris had been killed. This, then, was the situation: inside, these two fugitives, watchful, silent, their eyes red-rimmed for lack of sleep, their nerves raw and tingling as though rasped with files, each busy with certain private plans, each fighting off constantly the touch of the nasty scavenger flies that flickered and flitted iridescently about them; outside, in the steamy, hot drizzle, with his back to the locked and double-locked door, a leg-weary policeman, believing that he guarded a house all empty except for such evidences as yet remained of the Gilmorris murder.

It was one of those small, chancy things that so often disarrange the best laid plots of murderers that had dished their hope of a clean getaway and brought them back, at the last, to the starting point. If the plumber's helper, who was sent to cure a bathtub of leaking in the house next door, had not made a mistake and come to the wrong number; and if they, in the haste of flight, had not left an area door unfastened; and if this young plumbing apprentice, stumbling his way upstairs on the hunt for the misbehaving drain, had not opened the white enameled door and found inside there what he did find — if this small sequence of incidents had not occurred as it did and when it did, or if only it had been delayed another twenty-four hours, or even twelve, everything might have turned out differently. But fate, to call it by its fancy name — coincidence, to use its garden one — interfered, as it usually does in cases such as this. And so here they were.

The man had been on his way to the steamship office to get the tickets when an eruption of newsboys boiled out of Mail Street into Broadway, with extras on their arms, all shouting out certain words that sent him scurrying back in a panic to the small, obscure family hotel in the lower thirties where the woman waited. From that moment it was she, really, who took the initiative in all the efforts to break through the doubled and tripled lines that the police machinery looped about the five boroughs of the city.

At dark that evening "Mr. and Mrs. A. Thompson, of Jersey City," a quiet couple who went closely muffled up, considering that it was August, and carrying heavy valises, took quarters at a dingy furnished room house on a miscalled avenue of Brooklyn not far from the Wall Street ferries and overlooking the East River waterfront from its bleary back windows. Two hours later a very different-looking pair issued quietly from a side entrance of this place and vanished swiftly down toward the docks. The thing was well devised and carried out well too; yet by morning the detectives, already ranging and quartering the town as bird-dogs quarter a brier-field, had caught up again and pieced together the broken ends of the trail; and, thanks to them and the newspapers, a good many thousand wide awake persons were on the lookout for a plump, brown-skinned young woman with a cast in her right eye, wearing a boy's disguise and accompanied by a slender little man carrying his head slightly to one side, who when last seen wore smoked glasses and had his face extensively bandaged, as though suffering from a toothache.

Then had followed days and nights of blind twisting and dodging and hiding, with the hunt growing warmer behind them all the time. Through this they were guided and at times aided by things printed in the very papers that worked the hardest to run them down. Once they ventured as far as the outer entrance of the great, new uptown terminal, and turned away, too far gone and sick with fear to dare run the gauntlet of the waiting room and the train-shed. Once — because they saw a made-up Central Office man in every lounging long-shoreman, and were not so far wrong either — they halted at the street end of one of the smaller piers and from there watched a grimy little foreign boat that carried no wireless masts and that might have taken them to any one of half a dozen obscure banana ports of South America — watched her while she hiccoughed out into midstream and straightened down the river for the open bay — watched her out of sight and then fled again to their newest hiding place in the lower East Side in a cold sweat, with the feeling that every casual eye glance from every chance passer-by carried suspicion and recognition in its flash, that every briskening footstep on the pavement behind them meant pursuit.

Once in that tormented journey there was a sudden jingle of metal, like rattling handcuffs, in the man's ear and a heavy hand fell detainingly on his shoulder — and he squeaked like a caught shore-bird and shrunk away from under the rough grips of a truckman who had yanked him clear of a lurching truck horse tangled in its own traces. Then, finally, had come a growing distrust for their latest landlord, a stolid Russian Jew who read no papers and knew no English, and saw in his pale pair of guests only an American lady and gentleman who kept much to their room and paid well in advance for everything; and after that, in the hot rainy night, the flight afoot across weary miles of soaking cross streets and up through ill-lighted, shabby avenues to the one place of refuge left open to them. They had learned from the newspapers, at once a guide and a bane, a friend and a dogging enemy, that the place was locked up, now that the police had got through searching it, and that the coroner's people held the keys. And the woman knew of a faulty catch on a rear cellar window, and so, in a fit of stark desperation bordering on lunacy, back they ran, like a pair of spent foxes circling to a burrow from which they have been smoked out.

Again it was the woman who picked for her companion the easiest path through the inky-black alley, and with her own hands she pulled down noiselessly the broken slats of the rotting wooden wall at the back of the house. And then, soon, they were inside, with the reeking heat of the boxed-up house and the knowledge that at any moment discovery might come bursting in upon them — inside with their busy thoughts and the busy green flies. How persistent the things were — shake them off a hundred times and back they came buzzing! And where had they all come from? There had been none of them about before, surely, and now their maddening, everlasting droning filled the ear. And what nasty creatures they were, forever cleaning their shiny wings and rubbing the ends of their forelegs together with the loathsome suggestion of little grave-diggers anointing their palms. To the woman, at least, these flies almost made bearable the realization that, at best, this stopping point could be only a temporary one, and that within a few hours a fresh start must somehow be made, with fresh dangers to face at every turning.

It was during this last hideous day of flight and terror that the thing which had been growing in the back part of the brain of each of them began to assume shape and a definite aspect. The man had the craftier mind, but the woman had a woman's intuition, and she already had read his thoughts while yet he had no clue to hers. For the primal instinct of self-preservation, blazing up high, had burned away the bond of bogus love that held them together while they were putting her drunkard of a husband out of the way, and now there only remained to tie them fast this partnership of a common guilt.

In these last few hours they had both come to know that together there was no chance of ultimate escape; traveling together the very disparity of their compared appearances marked them with a fatal and unmistakable conspicuousness, as though they were daubed with red paint from the same paint brush; staying together meant ruin — certain, sure. Now, then, separated and going singly, there might be a thin strand of hope. Yet the man felt that, parted a single hour from the woman, and she still alive, his wofully small prospect would diminish and shrink to the vanishing point — New York juries being most notoriously easy upon women murderers who give themselves up and turn state's evidence; and, by the same mistaken processes of judgment, notoriously hard upon their male accomplices — half a dozen such instances had been playing in flashes across his memory already.

Neither had so much as hinted at separating. The man didn't speak, because of a certain idea that had worked itself all out hours before within his side-flattened skull. The woman likewise had refrained from putting in words the suggestion that had been uppermost in her brain from the time they broke into the locked house. Some darting look of quick, malignant suspicion from him, some inner warning sense, held her mute at first; and later, as the newborn hate and dread of him grew and mastered her and she began to canvass ways and means to a certain end, she stayed mute still.

Whatever was to be done must be done quietly, without a struggle — the least sound might arouse the policeman at the door below. One thing was in her favor — she knew he was not armed; he had the contempt and the fear of a tried and proved poisoner for cruder lethal tools.

It was characteristic also of the difference between these two that Devine should have had his plan stage-set and put to motion long before the woman dreamed of acting. It was all within his orderly scheme of the thing proposed that he, a shrinking coward, should have set his squirrel teeth hard and risked detection twice in that night: once to buy a basket of overripe fruit from a dripping Italian at a sidewalk stand, taking care to get some peaches — he just must have a peach, he had explained to her; and once again when he entered a dark little store on Second Avenue, where liquors were sold in their original packages, and bought from a sleepy, stupid clerk two bottles of a cheap domestic champagne — "to give us the strength for making a fresh start," he told her glibly, as an excuse for taking this second risk. So, then, with the third essential already resting at the bottom of an inner waistcoat pocket, he was prepared; and he had been waiting for his opportunity from the moment when they crept in through the basement window and felt their way along, she resolutely leading, to the windowless, shrouded middle room here on the second floor.

How she hated him, feared him too! He could munch his peaches and uncork his warm, cheap wine in this very room, with that bathroom just yonder and these flies all about. From under her fingers, interlaced over her forehead, her eyes roved past him, searching the littered room for the twentieth time in the hour, looking, seeking — and suddenly they fell on something — a crushed and rumpled hat of her own, a milliner's masterpiece, laden with florid plumage, lying almost behind him on a couch end where some prying detective had dropped it, with a big, round black button shining dully from the midst of its damaged tulle crown. She knew that button well. It was the imitation-jet head of a hatpin — a steel hatpin — that was ten inches long and maybe longer.

She looked and looked at the round, dull knob, like a mystic held by a hypnotist's crystal ball, and she began to breathe a little faster; she could feel her resolution tighten within her like a turning screw.

Beneath her brows, heavy and thick for a woman's, her eyes flitted back to the man. With the careful affectation of doing nothing at all, a theatricalism that she detected instantly, but for which she could guess no reason, he was cutting away at the damp, close-gnawed seed of the peach, trying apparently to fashion some little trinket — a toy basket, possibly — from it. His fingers moved deftly over its slick, wet surface. He had already poured out some of the champagne. One of the pint bottles stood empty, with the distorted button-headed cork lying beside it, and in two glasses the yellow wine was fast going flat and dead in that stifling heat. It still spat up a few little bubbles to the surface, as though minute creatures were drowning in it down below. The man was sweating more than ever, so that, under the single, low-turned gas jet, his crooked face had a greasy shine to it. A church clock down in the next block struck twelve slowly. The sleepless flies buzzed evilly.

"Look out again, won't you?" he said for perhaps the tenth time in two hours. "There's a chance, you know, that he might be gone — just a bare chance. And be sure you close the door into the hall behind you," he added as if by an afterthought. "You left it ajar once — this light might show through the window draperies."

At his bidding she rose more willingly than at any time before. To reach the door she passed within a foot of the end of the couch, and watching over her shoulder at his hunched-up back she paused there for the smallest fraction of time. The damaged picture hat slid off on the floor with a soft little thud, but he never turned around.

The instant, though, that the hall door closed behind her the man's hands became briskly active. He fumbled in an inner pocket of his unbuttoned waistcoat; then his right hand, holding a small cylindrical vial of a colorless liquid, passed swiftly over one of the two glasses of slaking champagne and hovered there a second. A few tiny globules fell dimpling into the top of the yellow wine, then vanished; a heavy reek, like the smell of crushed peach kernels, spread through the whole room. In the same motion almost he recorked the little bottle, stowed it out of sight, and with a quick, wrenching thrust that bent the small blade of his penknife in its socket he split the peach seed in two lengthwise and with his thumb-nail bruised the small brown kernel lying snugly within. He dropped the knife and the halved seed and began sipping at the undoctored glass of champagne, not forgetting even then to wave his fingers above it to keep the winged green tormentors out.

The door at the front reopened and the woman came in. Her thoughts were not upon smells, but instinctively she sniffed at the thick scent on the poisoned air.

"I accidentally split this peach seed open," he said quickly, with an elaborate explanatory air. "Stenches up the whole place, don't it? Come, take that other glass of champagne — it will do you good to —"

Perhaps it was some subtle sixth sense that warned him; perhaps the lightning-quick realization that she had moved right alongside him, poised and set to strike. At any rate he started to fling up his head — too late! The needle point of the jet-headed hatpin entered exactly at the outer corner of his right eye and passed backward for nearly its full length into his brain — smoothly, painlessly, swiftly. He gave a little surprised gasp, almost like a sob, and lolled his head back against the chair rest, like a man who has grown suddenly tired. The hand that held the champagne glass relaxed naturally and the glass turned over on its side with a small tinkling sound and spilled its thin contents on the table.

It had been easier than she had thought it would be. She stepped back, still holding the hatpin. She moved around from behind him, and then she saw his face, half upturned, almost directly beneath the low light. There was no blood, no sign even of the wound, but his jaw had dropped down unpleasantly, showing the ends of his lower front teeth, and his eyes stared up unwinkingly with a puzzled, almost a disappointed, look in them. A green fly lit at the outer corner of his right eye; more green flies were coming. And he didn't put up his hand to brush it away. He let it stay — he let it stay there.

With her eyes still fixed on his face, the woman reached out, feeling for her glass of the champagne. She felt that she needed it now, and at a gulp she took a good half of it down her throat.

She put the glass down steadily enough on the table; but into her eyes came the same puzzled, baffled look that his wore, and almost gently she slipped down into the chair facing him.

Then her jaw lolled a little too, and some of the other flies came buzzing toward her.

IV

ANOTHER OF THOSE CUB
REPORTER STORIES

The first time I saw Major Putnam Stone I didn't see him first. To be exact, I heard him first, and then I walked round the end of a seven-foot partition and saw him.

I had just gone to work for the Evening Press. As I recall now it was my second day, and I hadn't begun to feel at home there yet, and probably was more sensitive to outside sights and noises than I would ever again be in that place. Generally speaking, when a reporter settles down to his knitting, which in his case is his writing, he becomes impervious to all disturbances excepting those that occur inside his own brainpan. If he couldn't, he wouldn't amount to shucks in his trade. Give him a good, live-action story to write for an edition going to press in about nine minutes, and the rattles and slams of half a dozen typewriting machines, and the blattings of a pestered city editor, and the gabble of a couple of copy boys at his elbow, and all the rest of it won't worry him. He may not think he hears it, but he does, only instead of being distracting it is stimulating. It's all a part of the mechanism of the shop, helping him along unconsciously to speed and efficiency. I've often thought that, when I was handling a good, bloody murder story, say, it would tone up my style to have a phonograph about ten feet away grinding out The Last Ravings of John McCullough. Anyway, I am sure it wouldn't do any harm. A brass band playing a John Philip Sousa march makes fine accompaniment to write copy to. I've done it before now, covering parades and conventions, and I know.

But on this particular occasion I was, as I say, new to the job and maybe a little nervous to boot, and as I sat there, trying to frame a snappy opening paragraph for the interview I had just brought back with me from one of the hotels, I became aware of a voice somewhere in the immediate vicinity, a voice that didn't jibe in with my thoughts. At the moment I stopped to listen it was saying: "As for me, sir, I have always contended that the ultimate fate of the cause was due in great measure to the death of Albert Sidney Johnston at Shiloh on the evening of the first day's fight. Now then, what would have been the final result if Albert Sidney Johnston had lived? I ask you, gentlemen, what would have been the final result if Albert Sidney Johnston had lived?"

Across the room from me I heard Devore give a hollow groan. His desk was backed right up against the cross partition, and the partition was built of thin pine boards and was like a sounding board in his ear. Devore was city editor.

"Oh, thunder!" he said, half under his breath, "I'll be the goat! What would have been the result if Albert Sidney Johnston had lived?" He looked at me and gave a wink of serio-comic despair, and then he ran his blue pencil up through his hair and left a blue streak like a scar on his scalp. Devore was one of the few city editors I have ever seen who used that tool which all of them are popularly supposed to handle so murderously — a blue pencil. And as he had a habit, when he was flustered or annoyed — and that was most of the time — of scratching his head with the point end of it, his forehead under the hair roots was usually streaked with purplish-blue tracings, like a fly-catcher's egg.

The voice, which had a deep and space-filling quality to it, continued to come through and over the partition that divided off our cubby-hole of a workroom — called a city room by courtesy — from the space where certain other members of the staff had their desks. I got up from my place and stepped over to where the thin wall ended in a doorway, being minded to have a look at the speaker. The voice sounded as though it must belong to a big man with a barrel-organ chest. I was surprised to find that it didn't.

Its owner was sitting in a chair in the middle of a little space cluttered up with discarded exchanges and galley proofs. He was rather a small man, short but compact. He had his hat off and his hair, which was thin but fine as silk floss, was combed back over his ears and sprayed out behind in a sort of mane effect. It had been red hair once, but was now so thickly streaked with white that it had become a faded brindle color. I took notice of this first because his back was toward me; in a second or two he turned his head sideways and I saw that he had exactly the face to match the hair. It was a round, plump, elderly face, with a short nose, delicately pink at the tip. The eyes were a pale blue, and just under the lower lip, which protruded slightly, was a small gray-red goatee, sticking straight out from a cleft in the chin like a dab of a sandy sheep's wool. Also, as the speaker swung himself further round, I took note of a shirt of plaited white linen billowing out over his chest and ending at the top in a starchy yet rumply collar that rolled majestically and Byronically clear up under his ears. Under the collar was loosely knotted a black-silk tie such as sailors wear. His vest was unbuttoned, all except the two lowermost buttons, and the sleeves of his coat were turned back neatly off his wrists. This, though, could not have been on account of the heat, because the weather wasn't very hot yet. I learned later that, winter or summer, he always kept his coat sleeves turned back and the upper buttons of his vest unfastened. His hands were small and plump, and his feet were small too and daintily shod in low, square-toed shoes. About the whole man there was an air somehow of full-bloomed foppishness gone to tassel — as though having been a dandy once, he was now merely neat and precise in his way of dress.

He was talking along with the death of Albert Sidney Johnston for his subject, not seeming to notice that his audience wasn't deeply interested. He had, it seemed, a way of stating a proposition as a fact, as an indisputable, everlasting, eternal fact, an immutable thing. It became immutable through his way of stating it. Then he would frame it in the form of a question and ask it. Then he would answer it himself and go right ahead.

Boynton, the managing editor, was coiled up at his desk, wearing a look of patient endurance on his face. Harty, the telegraph editor, was trying to do his work — trying, I say, because the orator was booming away like a bittern within three feet of him and Harty plainly was pestered and fretful. Really the only person in sight who seemed entertained was Sidley, the exchange editor, a young man with hair that had turned white before its time and in his eye the devil-driven look of a man who drinks hard, not because he wants to drink but because he can't help drinking. Sidley, as I was to find out later, had less cause to care for the old man than anybody about the shop, for he used to disarrange Sidley's neatly piled exchanges, pawing through them for his favorite papers. But Sidley could forget his own grievances in watchful enjoyment of the dumb sufferings of Harty, whom he hated, as I came to know, with the blind hate a dipsomaniac often has for any mild and perfectly harmless individual.

As I stood there taking in the picture, the speaker, sensing a stranger's presence, faced clear about and saw me. He nodded with a grave courtesy, and then paused a moment as though expecting that one of the others would introduce us. None of the others did introduce us though, so he went ahead talking about Albert Sidney Johnston's death, and I turned away. I stopped by Devore's desk.

"Who is he?" I asked.

"That," he said, with a kind of leashed and restrained ferocity in his voice, "is Major Putnam P. Stone — and the P stands for Pest, which is his middle name — late of the Southern Confederacy."

"Picturesque-looking old fellow, isn't he?" I said.

"Picturesque old nuisance," he said, and jabbed at his scalp with his pencil as though he meant to puncture his skull. "Wait until you've been here a few weeks and you'll have another name for him."

"Well, anyway, he's got a good carrying voice," I said, rather at a loss to understand Devore's bitterness.

"Great," he mocked venomously; "you can hear it a mile. I hear it in my sleep. So will you when you get to know him, the old bore!"

In due time I did get to know Major Stone well. He was dignified, tiresome, conversational, gentle mannered and, I think, rather lonely. By driblets, a scrap here and a scrap there, I learned something about his private life. He came from the extreme eastern end of the state. He belonged to an old family. His grandfather — or maybe it was his great-grand-uncle — had been one of the first United States senators that went to Washington after our state was admitted into the Union. He had never married. He had no business or profession. From some property or other he drew an income, small, but enough to keep him in a sort of simple and genteel poverty. He belonged to the best club in town and the most exclusive, the Shawnee Club, and he had served four years in the Confederate army. That last was the one big thing in his life. To the major's conceptions everything that happened before 1861 had been of a preparatory nature, leading up to and paving the way for the main event; and what had happened since 1865 was of no consequence, except in so far as it reflected the effects of the Civil War.

Daily, as methodically as a milkwagon horse, he covered the same route. First he sat in the reading room of the old Gaunt House, where by an open fire in winter or by an open window in summer he discussed the blunders of Braxton Bragg and similar congenial topics with a little group of aging, fading, testy veterans. On his way to the Shawnee Club he would come by the Evening Press office and stay an hour, or two hours, or three hours, to go away finally with a couple of favored exchanges tucked under his arm, and leave us with our ears still dinned and tingling. Once in a while of a night, passing the Gaunt House on my way to the boarding house where I lived — for four dollars a week — I would see him through the windows, sometimes sitting alone, sometimes with one of his cronies.

Round the office he sometimes bothered us and sometimes he interfered with our work; but mainly all the men on the staff liked him, I think, or at least we put up with him. In our home town each of us had known somebody very much like him — there used to be at least one Major Stone in every community in the South, although most of them are dead now, I guess — so we all could understand him. When I say all I mean all but Devore. The major's mere presence would poison Devore's whole day for him. The major's blaring notes would cross-cut Devore's nerves as with a dull and haggling saw. He — Devore I mean — disliked the major with a dislike almost too deep for words. It had got to be an obsession with him.

"You fellows that were born down here have to stand for him," he said once, when the major had stumped out on his short legs after an unusually long visit. "It's part of the penalty you pay for belonging in this country. But I don't have to venerate him and fuss over him and listen to him. I'm a Yankee, thank the Lord!" Devore came from Michigan and had worked on papers in Cleveland and Detroit before he drifted South. "Oh, we've got his counterpart up my way," he went on. "Up there he'd be a pension-grabbing old kicker, ready to have a fit any time anybody wearing a gray uniform got within ninety miles of him, and writing red-hot letters of protest to the newspapers every time the state authorities sent a captured battle flag back down South. Down here he's a pompous, noisy old fraud, too proud to work for a living — or too lazy — and too poor to count for anything in this world. The difference is that up in my country we've squelched the breed — we got good and tired of these professional Bloody Shirt wavers a good while ago; but here you fuss over this man, and you'll sit round and pretend to listen while he drools away about things that happened before any one of you was born. Do you fellows know what I've found out about your Major Putnam Stone? He's a life member of the Shawnee Club — a life member, mind you! And here I've been living in this town over a year, and nobody ever so much as invited me inside its front door!"

All of which was, perhaps, true, even though Devore had an unnecessarily harsh way of stating the case; the part about the Shawnee Club was true, at any rate, and I used to think it possibly had something to do with Devore's feelings for Major Stone. Not that Devore gave open utterance to his feelings to the major's face. To the major he was always silently polite, with a little edging of ice on his politeness; he saved up his spleen to spew it out behind the old fellow's back. Farther than that he couldn't well afford to go anyhow. The Chief, owner of the paper and its editor, was the major's friend. As for the major himself, he seemed never to notice Devore's attitude. For a fact, I believe he actually felt a sort of pity for Devore, seeing that Devore had been born in the North. Not to have been born in the South was, from the major's way of looking at the thing, a great and regrettable misfortune for which the victim could not be held responsible, since the fault lay with his parents and not with him. By way of a suitable return for this, Devore spent many a spare moment thinking up grotesque yet wickedly appropriate nicknames for the major. He called him Old First and Second Manassas and

Old Hardee's Tactics and Old Valley of Virginia. He called him an old bluffer too.

He was wrong there, though, certainly. Though the major talked pretty exclusively about the war, I took notice that he rarely talked about the part he himself had played in it. Indeed, he rarely discussed anybody below the rank of brigadier. The errors of Hood's campaign concerned him more deeply than the personal performances of any individual. Campaigns you might say were his specialty, campaigns and strategy. About such things as these he could talk for hours — and he did.

I've known other men — plenty of them — not nearly so well educated as the major, who could tell you tales of the war that would make you see it — yes, and smell it too — the smoke of the campfires, the unutterable fatigue of forced marches when the men, with their tongues lolling out of their mouths like dogs, staggered along, panting like dogs; the bloody prints of unshod feet on flinty, frozen clods; the shock and fearful joy of the fighting; the shamed numbness of retreats; artillery horses, their hides all blood-boltered and their tails clubbed and clotted with mire, lying dead with stiff legs between overturned guns; dead men piled in heaps and living men huddled in panics — all of it. But when the major talked I saw only some serious-minded officers, in whiskers of an obsolete cut and queer-looking shirt collars, poring over maps round a table in a farmhouse parlor. When he chewed on the cud of the vanished past it certainly was mighty dry chewing.

There came a day, a few weeks after I went to work for the Evening Press, when for once anyway the major didn't seem to have anything to say. It was in the middle of a blistering, smothering hot forenoon in early June, muggy and still and close, when a fellow breathing felt as though he had his nose buried in layers of damp cotton waste. The city room was a place fit to addle eggs, and from the composing room at the back the stenches of melting metals and stale machine oils came rolling in to us in nasty waves. With his face glistening through the trickling sweat, the major came in about ten o'clock, fanning himself with his hat, and when he spoke his greeting the booming note seemed all melted and gone out of his voice. He went through the city room into the room behind the partition, and passing through a minute later I saw him sitting there with one of Sidley's exchanges unfolded across his knee, but he wasn't reading it. Presently I saw him climbing laboriously up the stairs to the second floor where the chief had his office. At quitting time that afternoon I dropped into the place on the corner for a beer, and I was drinking it, as close to an electric fan as I could get, when Devore came in and made for where I was standing. I asked him to have something.

"I'll take the same," he said to the man behind the bar, and then to me with a kind of explosive snap: "By George, I'm in a good mind to resign this rotten job!" That didn't startle me. I had been in the business long enough to know that the average newspaper man is forever threatening to resign. Most of them — to hear them talk — are always just on the point of throwing up their jobs and buying a good-paying country weekly somewhere and taking things easy for the rest of their lives, or else they're going into magazine work. Only they hardly ever do it. So Devore's threat didn't jar me much. I'd heard it too often.

"What's the trouble?" I asked. "Heat getting on your nerves?"

"No, it's not the heat," he said peevishly; "it's worse than the heat. Do you know what's happened? The chief has saddled Old Signal Corps on me. Yes, sir, I've got to take his old pet, the major, on the city staff. It seems he's succeeded in losing what little property he had — the chief told me some rigmarole about sudden financial reverses — and now he's down and out. So I'm elected. I've got to take him on as a reporter — a cub reporter sixty-odd years old, mind you, who hasn't heard of anything worth while since Robert E. Lee surrendered!"

The pathos of the situation — if you could call it that — hit me with a jolt; but it hadn't hit Devore, that was plain. He saw only the annoying part of it.

"What's he going to do?" I asked — "assignments, or cover a route like the district men?"

"Lord knows," said Devore. "Because the old bore knows a lot of big people in this town and is friendly with all the old-timers in the state, the chief has a wild delusion that he can pick up a lot of stuff that an ordinary reporter wouldn't get. Rats!

"Come on, let's take another beer," he said, and then he added: "Well, I'll just make you two predictions. He'll be a total loss as a reporter — that's one prediction; and the other is that he'll have a hard time buying his provender and his toddies over at the Shawnee Club on the salary he'll draw down from the Evening Press."

Devore was not such a very great city editor, as I know now in the light of fuller experience, but I must say that as a prophet he was fairly accurate. The major did have a hard time living on his salary — it was twelve a week, I learned — and as a reporter he certainly was not what you would call a dazzling success. He came on for duty at eight the next morning, the same as the rest of us, and sorry as I felt for him I had to laugh. He had bought himself a leather-backed notebook as big as a young ledger, just as a green kid just out of high school would have done, and he had a long, new, shiny, freshly sharpened lead pencil sticking out of the breast pocket of his coat. He tried to come in smartly with a businesslike air, but it wouldn't have fooled a blind man, because he was as nervous as a debutante. It struck me as one of the funniest things — and one of the most pathetic — I had ever seen.

I'll say this for Devore — he tried out the major on nearly every kind of job; and surely it wasn't Devore's fault that the major failed on every single one of them. His first attempt was as typical a failure as any of them. That first morning Devore assigned him to cover a wedding at high noon, high noon being the phrase we always used for a wedding that took place round twelve o'clock in the day. The daughter of one of the wealthiest merchants in the town, and also one of our largest advertisers, was going to be married to the first deputy cotillion leader of the German Club, or something of that nature. Anyhow the groom was what is known as prominent in society, and the chief wanted a spread made of it. Devore sent the major out to cover the wedding, and when he came back told him to write about half a column.

He wrote half a column before he mentioned the bride's name. He started off with an eight-line quotation from Walter Scott's Lady of the Lake, and then he went into a long, flowery dissertation on the sacred rite or ceremony of matrimony, proving conclusively and beyond the peradventure of a doubt that it was handed down to us from remote antiquity. And he forgot altogether to tell the minister's name, and he got the groom's middle initial wrong — he was the kind of groom who would make a fuss over a wrong middle initial, too — and along toward the end of his story he devoted about three closely-written pages to the military history of the young woman's father. It seems that her parent had served with distinction as colonel of a North Carolina regiment. And he wound up with a fancy flourish and handed it in. I know all these details of his story, because it fell to me to rewrite it.

Devore didn't say a word when the old major reverently laid that armload of copy down in front of him. He just sat and waited in silence until the major had gone out to get a bite to eat, and then he undertook to edit it. But there wasn't any way to edit it, except to throw it away. I suppose that kind of literature went very well indeed back along about 1850; I remember having read such accounts in the back files of old weeklies, printed before the war. But we were getting out a live, snappy paper. Devore tried to pattern the local side after the New York and Chicago models. As yet we hadn't reached the point where we spoke of any white woman without the prefix Mrs. or Miss before her name, but we were up-to-date in a good many other particulars. Why, it was even against the office rule to run "beauty and chivalry" into a story when describing a mixed assemblage of men and women; and when a Southern newspaper bars out that ancient and honorable standby among phrases it is a sign that the old order has changed.

For ten minutes or so Devore, cursing softly to himself, cut and chopped and gutted his way through the major's introduction, and between slashing strokes made a war map of the Balkans in his scalp with his blue pencil. Then he lost patience altogether.

"Here," he said to me, "you're not doing anything, are you? Well, take this awful bunch of mushy slush and read it through, and then try to make a decent half-column story out of it. And rush it over a page at a time, will you? We've got to hustle to catch the three o'clock edition with it."

Long before three o'clock the major was back in the shop, waiting for the first run of papers to come off the press. Furtively I watched him as he hunted through the sticky pages to find his first story. I guess he had the budding pride of authorship in him, just as all the rest of us have it in us. But he didn't find his story, he found mine. He didn't say anything, but he looked crushed and forlorn as he got up and went away. It was like him not to ask for any explanations, and it was like Devore not to offer him any.

So it went. Even if he had grown up in the business I doubt whether Major Putnam Stone would ever have made a newspaper man; and now he was too far along in life to pick up even the rudiments of the trade. He didn't have any more idea of news values than a rabbit. He had the most amazing faculty for overlooking what was vital in the news, but he could always be depended upon to pick out some trivial and inconsequential detail and dress it up with about half a yard of old-point lace adjectives. He never by any chance used a short word if he could dig up a long, hard one, and he never seemed to be able to start a story without a quotation from one of the poets. It never was a modern poet either. Excepting for Sidney Lanier and Father Ryan, apparently he hadn't heard of any poet worth while since Edgar Allan Poe died. And everything that happened seemed to remind him — at great length — of something else that had happened between 1861 and 1865. When it came to lugging the Civil War into a tale, he was as bad as that character in one of Dickens' novels who couldn't keep the head of King Charles the First out of his literary productions. With that reared-back, flat-heeled, stiff-spined gait of his, he would go rummaging round the hotels and the Shawnee Club, meeting all sorts of people and hearing all sorts of things that a real reporter would have snatched at like a hungry dog snatching at a T-bone, and then he would remember that it was the fortieth anniversary of the Battle of Kenesaw Mountain, or something, and, forgetting everything else, would come bulging and bustling back to the office, all worked up over the prospect of writing two or three columns about that. He just simply couldn't get the viewpoint; yet I think he tried hard enough. I guess the man who said you couldn't teach an old dog new tricks had particular reference to an old war dog.

I remember mighty well one incident that illustrates the point I am trying to make. We had a Sunday edition. We were rather vain of our Sunday edition. It carried a colored comic supplement and a section full of special features, and we all took a more or less righteous pride in it and tried hard to make it alive and attractive. We didn't always succeed, but we tried all right. One Saturday night we put the Sunday to bed, and about one o'clock, when the last form was locked, three or four of us dropped into Tony's place at the corner for a bite to eat and a drink. We hadn't been there very long when in came the old major, and at my invitation he joined us at one of Tony's little round tables at the back of the place. As a general thing the major didn't patronize Tony's. I had never heard him say so — probably he wouldn't have said it for fear of hurting our feelings — but I somehow had gathered the impression that the major believed a gentleman, if he drank at all, should drink at his club. But it was long after midnight now and the Shawnee Club would be closed. Ike Webb spoke up presently.

"It's a pity we couldn't dig up the governor tonight," he said.

The governor had come down from the state capital about noon, and all the afternoon and during most of the evening Webb had been trying to find him. There was a possibility of a big story in the governor if Webb could have found him. The major, who had been sitting there stirring his toddy in an absent-minded sort of way, spoke up casually: "I spent an hour with the governor tonight — at my club. In fact, I supped with him in one of the private dining rooms." We looked up, startled, but the major went right along. "Young gentlemen, it may interest you to know that every time I see our worthy governor I am struck more and more by his resemblance to General Leonidas Polk, as that gallant soldier and gentleman looked when I last saw him —"

Devore, who had been sitting next to the major, with his shoulder half turned from the old man, swung round sharply and interrupted him.

"Major," he said, with a thin icy stream of sarcasm trickling through his words, "did you and the governor by any remote chance discuss anything so brutally new and fresh as the present political complications in this state?"

"Oh, yes," said the major blandly. "We discussed them quite at some length — or at least the governor did. Personally I do not take a great interest in these matters, not so great an interest as I should, perhaps, take. However, I did feel impelled to take issue with him on one point. Our governor is an honest gentleman — more than that, he was a brave soldier — but I fear he is mistaken in some of his attitudes. I regard him as being badly advised. For example, he told me that no longer ago than this afternoon he affixed his official signature to a veto of Senator Stickney's measure in regard to the warehouses of our state —"

As Devore jumped up he overturned the major's toddy right in the major's lap. He didn't stop to beg pardon, though; in fact, none of us stopped. But at the door I threw one glance backward over my shoulder. The major was still sitting reared back in his chair, with his wasted toddy seeping all down the front of his billowy shirt, viewing our vanishing figures with amazement and a mild reproof in his eyes. In the one quick glance that I took I translated his expression to mean something like this:

"Good Heavens, is this any way for a party of gentlemen to break up! This could never happen at a gentlemen's club."

It was a foot-race back to the office, and Devore, who had the start, won by a short length. Luckily the distance was short, not quite half a block, and the presses hadn't started yet. Working like the crew of a sinking ship, we snatched the first page form back off the steam table and pried it open and gouged a double handful of hot slugs out of the last column — Devore blistered his fingers doing it. A couple of linotype operators who were on the late trick threw together the stick or two of copy that Webb and I scribbled off a line at a time. And while we were doing this Devore framed a triple-deck, black-face head. So we missed only one mail.

The first page had a ragged, sloppy look, but anyway we were saved from being scooped to death on the most important story of the year. The vetoing of the Stickney Bill vitally affected the tobacco interests, and they were the biggest interests in the state, and half the people of the state had been thinking about nothing else and talking about nothing else for two months — ever since the extra session of the legislature started. It was well for us too that we did save our faces, because the opposition sheet had managed to find the governor — he was stopping for the night at the house of a friend out in the suburbs — and over the telephone at a late hour he had announced his decision to them. But by Monday morning the major seemed to have forgotten the whole thing. I think he had even forgiven Devore for spilling his toddy and not stopping to apologize.

As for Devore, he didn't say a word to the major — what would have been the use? To Devore's credit also I will say that he didn't run to the chief, bearing complaints of the major's hopeless incompetency. He kept his tongue between his teeth and his teeth locked; and that must have been hard on Devore, for he was a flickery, high-tempered man, and nervous as a cat besides. To my knowledge, the only time he ever broke out was when we teetotally missed the Castleton divorce story. So far as the major's part in it was concerned, it was the Stickney veto story all over again, with variations. The Castletons were almost the richest people in town, and socially they stood way up. That made the scandal that had been brewing and steeping and simmering for months all the bigger when finally it came to a boil. When young Buford Castleton got his eyes open and became aware of what everybody else had known for a year or more, and when the rival evening paper came out in its last edition with the full particulars, we, over in the Evening Press shop, were plastered with shame, for we didn't have a line of it.

A stranger dropping in just about that time would have been justified in thinking there was a corpse laid out in the plant somewhere, and that all the members of the city staff were sitting up with the remains. As luck would have it, it wasn't a stranger that dropped in on our grand lodge of sorrow. It was Major Putnam Stone, and as he entered the door he caught the tag end of what one of us was saying.

"I gather," he said in that large round voice of his, "that you young gentlemen are discussing the unhappy affair which, I note, is mentioned with such signally poor taste in the columns of our sensational contemporary. I may state that I knew of this contemplated divorce action yesterday. Mr. Buford Castleton, Senior, was my informant."

"What!" Devore almost yelled it. He had the love of a true city editor for his paper, and the love of a mother for her child or a miser for his gold is no greater love than that, let me tell you. "You knew about this thing here?" He beat with two fingers that danced like the prongs of a tuning fork on the paper spread out in front of him. "You knew it yesterday?"

"Certainly," said the major. "The elder Mr. Castleton bared the truly distressing details to me at the Shawnee Club."

"In confidence though — he told you about it in confidence, didn't he, major?" said Ike Webb, trying to save the old fellow.

But the major besottedly wouldn't be saved.

"Absolutely not," he said. "There were several of us present, at least three other gentlemen whose names I cannot now recall. Mr. Castleton made the disclosure as though he wished it to be known among his friends and his son's friends. It was quite evident to all of us that he was entirely out of sympathy with the lady who is his daughter-in-law."

Devore forced himself to be calm. It was almost as though he sat on himself to hold himself down in his chair;

but when he spoke his voice ran up and down the scales quiveringly.

"Major," he said, "don't you think it would be a good idea if you would admit that the Southern Confederacy was defeated, and turned your attention to a few things that have occurred subsequently? Why didn't you write this story? Why didn't you tell me, so that I could write it? Why didn't — Oh, what's the use!"

The major straightened himself up.

"Sir," he said, "allow me to correct you in regard to a plain misstatement of fact. Sir, the Southern Confederacy was never defeated. It ceased to exist as a nation because we were exhausted — because our devastated country was exhausted. Another thing, sir, I am employed upon this paper, I gainsay you, as a reporter, not as a scandal monger. I would be the last to give circulation in the public prints to another gentleman's domestic unhappiness. I regard it as highly improper that a gentleman's private affairs should be aired in a newspaper under any circumstances."

And with that he bowed and turned on his heel and went out, leaving Devore shaking all over with the superhuman task of trying to hold himself in. About ten minutes later, when I came out bound for my boarding house, the major was standing at the front door. He looped one of his absurdly small fingers into one of my buttonholes.

"Our city editor means well, no doubt," he said, "but he doesn't understand, he doesn't appreciate our conceptions of these matters. He was born on the other side of the river, you know," he said as though that explained everything. Then his tone changed and anxiety crept into it. "Do you think that I went too far? Do you think I ought to return to him and apologize to him for the somewhat hasty and abrupt manner of speech I used just now?"

I told him no — I didn't know what might happen if he went back in there then — and I persuaded him that Devore didn't expect any apology; and with that he seemed better satisfied and walked off. As I stood there watching him, his stiff old back growing smaller as he went away from me, I didn't know which I blamed the more, Devore for his malignant, cold disdain of the major, or the major for his blatant stupidity. And right then and there, all of a sudden, there came to me an understanding of a thing that had been puzzling me all these weeks. Often I had wondered how the major had endured Devore's contempt. I had decided in my own mind that he must be blind to it, else he would have shown resentment. But now I knew the answer. The major wasn't blind, he was afraid; as the saying goes, he was afraid of his job. He needed it; he needed the little scrap of money it brought him every Saturday night. That was it, I knew now.

Knowing it made me sorrier than ever for the old man. Dimly I began to realize, I think, what his own mental attitude toward his position must be. Here he was, a mere cub reporter — and a remarkably bad one, a proven failure — skirmishing round for small, inconsequential items, running errands really, at an age when most of the men he knew were getting ready to retire from business. Yet he didn't dare quit. He didn't dare even to rebel against the slights of the man over him, because he needed that twelve dollars a week. It was all, no doubt, that stood between him and actual want. His pride was bleeding to death internally. On top of all that he was being forced into a readjustment of his whole scheme of things, at a time of life when its ordered routine was almost as much a part of him as his hands and feet. As I figured it, he had long before adjusted his life to his income, cunningly fitting in certain small luxuries and all the small comforts; and now this income was cut to a third or a quarter perhaps of its former dimensions. It seemed a pretty hard thing for the major. It was fierce.

Perhaps my vision was clouded by my sympathy, but I thought Major Stone aged visibly that summer. Maybe you have noticed how it is with men who have gone along, hale and stanch, until they reach a certain age. When they do start to break they break fast. He lost some of his flesh and most of his rosiness. The skin on his face loosened a little and became a tallowy yellowish-red, somewhat like a winter-killed apple.

His wardrobe suffered. One day one of his short little shoes was split across the top just back of the toe cap, and the next morning it was patched. Pretty soon the other shoe followed suit — first a crack in the leather, then a clumsy patch over the crack. He wore his black slouch hat until it was as green in spots as a gage plum; and late in August he supplanted it with one of those cheap, varnished brown-straw hats that cost about thirty-five cents apiece and look it.

His linen must have been one of his small extravagances. Those majestically collared garments with the tremendous plaited bosoms and the hand worked eyelets, where the three big flat gold studs went in, never came ready made from any shop. They must have been built to his measure and his order. Now he wore them until there were gaped places between the plaits where the fine, fragile linen had ripped lengthwise, and the collars were frayed down and broken across and caved in limply. Finally he gave them up too, and one morning came to work wearing a flimsy, sleazy, negligee shirt. I reckon you know the kind of shirt I mean — always it fits badly, and the sleeves are always short and the bosom is skimpy, and the color design is like bad wall-paper. After his old full-bosomed grandeur this shirt, with a ten-cent collar buttoned on to it and overriding the neckband, and gaping away in the front so that the major's throat showed, seemed to typify more than anything else the days upon which he had fallen. About this time I thought his voice took on a changed tone permanently. It was still hollow, but it no longer rang.

A good many men similarly placed would have taken to drink, but Major Putnam Stone plainly was never born to be a drunkard and hard times couldn't make one of him. With a sort of gentle, stupid persistence he hung fast to his poor job, blundering through some way, struggling constantly to learn the first easy tricks of the trade — the a, b, c's of it — and never succeeding. He still lugged the classical poets and the war into every story he tried to write, and day after day Devore maintained his policy of eloquent brutal silence, refusing dumbly to accept the major's clumsy placating attempts to get upon a better footing with him. After that once he had never attempted to scold the old man, but he would watch the major pottering round the city room, and he would chew on his under lip and viciously lance his scalp with his pencil point.

Well, aside from the major, Devore had his troubles that summer. That was the summer of the biggest, bitterest campaign that the state had seen, so old-timers said, since Breckinridge ran against Douglas and both of them against Lincoln. If you have ever lived in the South, probably you know something of political fights that will divide a state into two armed camps, getting hotter and hotter until old slumbering animosities come crawling out into the open, like poison snakes from under a rock, and new lively ones hatch from the shell every hour or so in a multiplying adder brood.

This was like that, only worse. Stripped of a lot of embroidery in the shape of side issues and local complications, it resolved itself in a last-ditch, last-stand, back-to-the-wall fight of the old régime of the party against the new. On one side were the oldsters, bearers of famous names some of them, who had learned politics as a trade and followed it as a profession. Almost to a man they were professional office holders, professional handshakers, professional silver tongues. And against them were pitted a greedy, hungry group of younger men, less showy perhaps in their persons, less picturesque in their manner of speech, but filled each one with a great yearning for office and power; and they brought to the aid of their vaulting ambitions a new and a faultlessly running machine. From the outset the Evening Press had championed the cause of the old crowd — the state-house ring as the enemy called it, when they didn't call it something worse. We championed it not as a Northern or an Eastern paper might, in a sedate, half-hearted way, but fiercely and wholly and blindly — so blindly that we could see nothing in our own faction but what was good and high and pure, nothing in the other but what was smutted with evil intent. In daily double-leaded editorial columns the chief preached a Holy War, and in the local pages we fought the foe tooth and nail, biting and gouging and clawing, and they gouged and clawed back at us like catamounts. That was where the hard work fell upon Devore. He had to keep half his scanty staff working on politics while the other half tried to cover the run of the news.

If I live to be a thousand years old I am not going to forget the state convention that began at two o'clock that muggy September afternoon at Lyric Hall up on Washington Street in the old part of the town. Once upon a time, twenty or thirty years before, Lyric Hall had been the biggest theater in town. The stage was still there and the boxes, and at the back there were miles — they seemed miles anyway — of ancient, crumbling, dauby scenery stacked up and smelling of age and decay. Booth and Barrett had played there, and Fanny Davenport and Billy Florence. Now, having fallen from its high estate, it served altered purposes — conventions were held at Lyric Hall and cheap masquerade balls and the like.

The press tables that had been provided were not, strictly speaking, press tables at all. They were ordinary unpainted kitchen tables, ranged two on one side and two on the other side at the front of the stage, close up to the old gas-tipped footlights; and when we came in by the back way that afternoon and found our appointed places I was struck by certain sinister facts. Usually women flocked to a state convention. By rights there should have been ladies in the boxes and in the balcony. Now there wasn't a woman in sight anywhere, only men, row after row of them. And there wasn't any cheering, or mighty little of it. When I tell you the band played Dixie all the way through with only a stray whoop now and then, you will understand better the temper of that crowd.

The situation, you see, was like this: One side had carried the mountain end of the state; the other had carried the lowlands. One side had swept the city; that meant a solid block of more than a hundred delegates. The other side had won the small towns and the inland counties. So it stood lowlander against highlander, city man against country man, and the bitter waters of those ancient feuds have their wellsprings back a thousand years in history, they tell me. One side led slenderly on instructed vote. The other side had enough contesting delegations on hand to upset the result if these contestants or any considerable proportion of them should be recognized in the preliminary organization.

One side held a majority of the delegates who sat upon the floor; the other side had packed the balcony and the aisles and the corners with its armed partizans. One side was in the saddle and determined; the other afoot and grimly desperate. And it was our side, as I shall call it, meaning by that the state-house ring, that for the moment had the whiphand; and it was the other side, led in person by State Senator Stickney, god of the new machine, that stood ready to wade hip deep through trouble to unhorse us.

Just below me, stretching across the hall from side to side in favored front places, sat the city delegates —

Stickney men all of them. And as my eye swept the curved double row of faces it seemed to me I saw there every man in town with a reputation as a gun-fighter or a knife-fighter or a fist-fighter; and every one of them wore, pinning his delegate's badge to his breast, a Stickney button that was round and bright red, like a clot of blood on his shirt front.

They made a contrast, these half-moon lines of blocky men, to the lank, slouch-hatted, low-collared country delegates — farmers, school teachers, country doctors and country lawyers — who filled the seats behind them and on beyond them. To the one group politics was a business in which there was money to be made and excitement to be had; to the other group it was a passion, veritably a sacredly high and serious thing, which they took as they did their religion, with a solemn, intolerant, Calvinistic sincerity. There was one thing, though, they all shared in common. Whether a man's coat was of black alpaca or striped flannel, the right-hand pocket sagged under the weight of unseen ironmongery; or if the coat pocket didn't sag there was a bulging clump back under the skirts on the right hip. For all the heat, hardly a man there was in his shirtsleeves; and it would have been funny to watch how carefully this man or that eased himself down into his seat, favoring his flanks against the pressure of his hardware — that is to say, it would have been funny if it all hadn't been so deadly earnest.

You could fairly smell trouble cooking in that hall. In any corner almost there were the potential makings of half a dozen prominent funerals. There was scarce a man, I judged, but nursed a private grudge against some other man; and then besides these there was the big issue itself, which had split the state apart lengthwise as a butcher's cleaver splits a joint. Looking out over that convention, you could read danger spelled out everywhere, in everything, as plain as print.

I was where I could read it with particular and uncomfortable distinctness, too, for I had the second place at the table that had been assigned to the Evening Press crew. There were four of us in all — Devore, who had elected to be in direct charge of the detail; Ike Webb, our star man, who was to handle the main story; I who was to write the running account — and, fourthly and lastly, Major Putnam Stone. The major hadn't been included in the assignment originally, but little Pinky Gilfoil had turned up sick that morning, and the chief decided the major should come along with us in Gilfoil's place. The chief had a deluded notion that the major could circulate on a roving commission and pick up spicy scraps of gossip. But here, for this once anyway, was a convention wherein there were no spicy bits of gossip to be picked up — curse words, yes, and cold-chilled fighting words, but not gossip — everything focused and was summed up in the one main point: Should the majority rule the machine or should the machine rule the majority? So the major sat there at the far inside corner of the table doing nothing at all — Devore saw to that — and was rather in the way. For the time I forgot all about him.

The clash wasn't long in coming. It came on the first roll call of the counties. Later we found out that the Stickney forces had been counting, all along, on throwing the convention into a disorder of such proportions as to force an adjournment, trusting then to their acknowledged superiority at organization to win some strong strategic advantage in the intervening gap of time. Failing there they meant to raise a cry of unfairness and walk out. That then was their program — first the riot and then, as a last resort, the bolt. But they had men in their ranks, high-tempered men who, like so many skittish colts, wouldn't stand without hitching. The signals crossed and the thunder cracked across that calm-before-the-storm situation before there was proper color of excuse either for attack or for retreat.

It came with scarcely any warning at all. Old Judge Marcellus Barbee, the state chairman, called the convention to order, he standing at a little table in the center of the stage. Although counted as our man, the judge was of such uncertain fiber as to render it doubtful whose man he really was. He was a kindly, wind-blown old gentleman, who very much against his will had been drawn unawares, as it were, into the middle of this fight, and he was bewildered by it all — and not only bewildered but unhappy and frightened. His gavel seemed to quaver its raps out timorously.

A pastor of one of the churches, a reverend man with a bleak, worried face, prayed the Good Lord that peace and good-will and wise counsel might rule these deliberations, and then fled away as though fearing the mocking echoes of his own Amen. Summoning his skulking voice out of his lower throat, Judge Barbee bade the secretary of the state committee call the counties. The secretary got as far as Blanton, the third county alphabetically down the list. And Blanton was one of the contested counties. So up rose two rival chairmen of delegations, each waving aloft his credentials, each demanding the right to cast the vote of free and sovereign Blanton, each shaking a clenched fist at the other. Up got the rival delegations from Blanton. Up got everybody. Judge Barbee, with a gesture, recognized the rights of the anti-Stickney delegation. Jeers and yells broke out, spattering forth like a skirmish fire, then almost instantly were merged into a vast, ominous roar. Chairs began to overturn. Not twenty feet from me the clattering of the chairman's gavel, as he vainly beat for order, sounded like the clicking of a telegraph instrument in a cyclone.

I saw the sergeant-at-arms — who was our man too — start down the middle aisle and saw him trip over a hostile leg and stumble and fall, and I saw a big mountaineer drop right on top of him, pinning him flat to the floor. I saw the musicians inside the orchestra rail, almost under my feet, scuttling away in two directions like a divided covey of gorgeous blue and red birds. I saw the snare drummer, a little round German, put his foot through the skin roof of his own drum. I saw Judge Barbee overturn the white china pitcher of ice water that sweated on the table at his elbow, and as the cold stream of its contents spattered down the legs of his trousers saw him staring downward, contemplating his drenched limbs as though that mattered greatly.

All in a flash I saw these things, and in that same flash I saw, taking shape and impulse, a groundswell of men, all wearing red buttons, rolling toward the stage, with the picked bad men of the city wards for its crest; and out of the tail of my eye I saw too, stealing out from the rear of the stage, a small, compact wedge of men wearing those same red buttons; and the prow of the wedge was Fighting Dave Dancy, the official bad man of a bad county, a man who packed a gun on each hip and carried a dirk knife down the back of his neck; a man who would shoot you at the drop of a hat and provide the hat himself — or at least so it was said of him.

And I realized that the enemy, coming by concerted agreement from front and rear at once, had nipped those of us who were upon the stage as between two closing walls, and I was exceedingly unhappy to be there. I ducked my head low, waiting for the shooting to begin. Afterward we figured it out that nobody fired the first shot because everybody knew the first shot would mean a massacre, where likely enough a man would kill more friends than foes.

What happened now in the space of the next few seconds I saw with particular clarity of vision, because it happened right alongside me and in part right over me. I recall in especial Mink Satterlee. Mink Satterlee was one of the worst men in town, and he ran the worst saloon and prevailed mightily in ward politics. He had been sitting just below our table in the front row of seats. He was a big-bodied man, fat-necked, but this day he showed himself quick on his feet as any toe-dancer. Leading his own forces by a length, he vaulted the orchestra rail and lit lightly where a scared oboe player had been squatted a moment before; Mink breasted the gutterlike edging of the footlights and leaped upward, teetering a moment in space. One of his hands grabbed out for a purchase and closed on the leg of our table and jerked it almost from under us.

At that Devore either lost his head or else indignation made him reckless. Still half sitting, he kicked out at the wriggling bulk at his feet, and the toe of his shoe took Mink Satterlee in his chest. It was a puny enough kick; it didn't even shake Mink Satterlee loose from where he clung. He gave a bellow and heaved himself up on the stage and, before any of us could move, grabbed Devore by the throat with his left hand and jammed him back, face upward, on the table until I thought Devore's spine would crack. His right hand shot into his coat pocket, then, quick as a snake, came out again, showing the fat fist armed with a set of murderously heavy brass knucks, and he bent his arm in a crooked sickle-like stroke, aiming for Devore's left temple. I've always been satisfied — and so has Devore — that if the blow had landed true his skull would have caved in like a puff-ball. Only it never landed.

Above me a shadow of something hung for the hundredth part of a second, something white flashed over me and by me, moving downward whizzingly; something cracked on something; and Mink Satterlee breathed a gentle little grunt right in Devore's face and then relaxed and slid down on the floor, lying half under the table and half in the tin trough where the stubby gas jets of the footlights stood up, with his legs protruding stiffly out over its edge toward his friends. Subconsciously I noted that his socks were not mates, one of them being blue and one black; also that his scalp had a crescent-shaped split place in it just between and above his half-closed eyes. All this, though, couldn't have taken one-fifth of the time it has required for me to tell it. It couldn't have taken more than a brace of seconds, but even so it was time enough for other things to happen; and I looked back again toward the center of the stage just as Fighting Dave Dancy seized startled old Judge Barbee by the middle from behind and flung him aside so roughly that the old man spun round twice, clutching at nothing, and then sat down very hard, yards away from where he started spinning.

Dancy stooped for the gavel, which had fallen from the judge's hand, being minded, I think, to run the convention awhile in the interest of his own crowd. But his greedy fingers never closed over its black-walnut handle, because, facing him, he saw just then what made him freeze solid where he was.

Out from behind the Evening Press table and through a scattering huddle of newspaper reporters, stepping on the balls of his feet as lightly as a puss-cat, emerged Major Putnam Stone. His sleeves were turned back off his wrists and his vest flared open. His head was thrust forward so that the tuft of goatee on his chin stuck straight out ahead of him like a little burgee in a fair breeze. His face was all a clear, bright, glowing pink; and in his right hand he held one of the longest cavalry revolvers that ever was made, I reckon. It had a square-butted ivory handle, and as I saw that ivory handle I knew what the white thing was that had flashed by me only a moment before to fell Mink Satterlee so expeditiously.

Writing this, I've been trying to think of the one word that would best describe how Major Putnam Stone looked to me as he advanced on Dave Dancy. I think now that the proper word is competent, for indeed the old major did look most competent — the tremendous efficiency he radiated filled him out and made him seem sundry sizes larger than he really was. A great emergency acts upon different men as chemical processes act upon different metals. Some it melts like lead, so that their resolution softens and runs away from them; and some it hardens to tempered steel. There was the old major now. Always before this he had seemed to me to be but pot metal and putty, and here, poised, alert, ready — a wire-drawn, hard-hammered Damascus blade of a man — all changed and transformed and glorified, he was coming down on Dave Dancy, finger on trigger, thumb on hammer, eye on target, dominating the whole scene.

Ten feet from him he halted and there was nobody between them. Somehow everybody else halted too, some even giving back a little. Over the edge of the stage a ring of staring faces, like a high-water mark, showed where the onward rushing swell of the Stickney city delegates had checked itself. Seemingly to all at once came the realization that the destinies of the fight had by the chances of the fight been entrusted to these two men — to Dancy and the major — and that between them the issue would be settled one way or the other.

Still at a half crouch, Dancy's right hand began to steal back under the skirt of his long black coat. At that the major flung up the muzzle of his weapon so that it pointed skyward, and he braced his left arm at his side in the attitude you have seen in the pictures of dueling scenes of olden times.

"I am waiting, sir, for you to draw," said the major quite briskly. "I will shoot it out with you to see whether right or might shall control this convention." And his heels clicked together like castanets.

Dancy's right hand kept stealing farther and farther back. And then you could mark by the change of his skin and by the look out of his eyes how his courage was clabbering to whey inside him, making his face a milky, curdled white, the color of a poorly stirred emulsion, and then he quit — he quit cold — his hand came out again from under his coat tails and it was an empty hand and wide open. It was from that moment on that throughout our state Fighting Dave Dancy ceased to be Fighting Dave and became instead Yaller Dave.

"Then, sir," said the major, "as you do not seem to care to shoot it out with me, man to man, you and your friends will kindly withdraw from this stage and allow the business of this convention to proceed in an orderly manner."

And as Dave Dancy started to go somebody laughed. In another second we were all laughing and the danger was over. When an American crowd begins laughing the danger is always over.

Newspaper men down in that town still talk about the story that Ike Webb wrote for the last edition of the Evening Press that afternoon. It was a great story, as Ike Webb told it — how, still sitting on the floor, old Judge Barbee got his wits back and by word of mouth commissioned the major a special sergeant-at-arms; how the major privily sent men to close and lock and hold the doors so that the Stickney people couldn't get out to bolt, even if they had now been of a mind to do so; how the convention, catching the spirit of the moment, elected the major its temporary chairman, and how even after that, for quite a spell, until some of his friends bethought to remove him, Mink Satterlee slept peacefully under our press table with his mismated legs bridged across the tin trough of the footlights.

In rapid succession a number of unusual events occurred in the Evening Press shop the next morning. To begin with, the chief came down early. He had a few words in private with Devore and went upstairs. When the major came at eight as usual, Devore was waiting for him at the door of the city room; and as they went upstairs together, side by side, I saw Devore's arm steal timidly out and rest a moment on the major's shoulder.

The major was the first to descend. Walking unusually erect, even for him, he bustled into the telephone booth. Jessie, our operator, told us afterward that he called up a haberdasher, and in a voice that boomed like a bell ordered fourteen of those plaited-bosom shirts of his, the same to be made up and delivered as soon as possible. Then he stalked out. And in a minute or two more Devore came down looking happy and unhappy and embarrassed and exalted, all of them at once. On his way to his desk he halted midway of the floor.

"Gentlemen," he said huskily — "fellows, I mean — I've got an announcement to make, or rather two announcements. One is this: Right here before you fellows who heard most of them I want to take back all the mean things I ever said about him — about Major Stone — and I want to say I'm sorry for all the mean things I've done to him. I've tried to beg his pardon, but he wouldn't listen — he wouldn't let me beg his pardon — he — he said everything was all right. That's one announcement. Here's the other: The major is going to have a new job with this paper. He's going to leave the city staff. Hereafter he's going to be upstairs in the room next to the chief. He's gone out now to pick out his own desk. He's going to write specials for the Sunday — specials about the war. And he's going to do it on a decent salary too."

I judge by my own feelings that we all wanted to cheer, but didn't because we thought it might sound theatrical and foolish. Anyhow, I know that was how I felt. So there was a little awkward pause.

"What's his new title going to be?" asked somebody then.

"The title is appropriate — I suggested it myself," said Devore. "Major Stone is going to be war editor."

V

SMOKE OF BATTLE

This befell during the period that Major Putnam Stone, at the age of sixty-two, held a job as cub reporter on the Evening Press and worked at it until his supply of fine linen and the patience of City Editor Wilbert Devore frazzled out practically together. The episode to which I would here direct attention came to pass in the middle of a particularly hot week in the middle of that particularly hot and grubby summer, at a time when the major was still wearing the last limp survivor of his once adequate stock of frill-bosomed, roll-collared shirts, and when Devore's scanty stock of endurance had already worn perilously near the snapping point.

As may be recalled, Major Stone lived a life of comparative leisure from the day he came out of the Confederate army, a seasoned veteran, until the day he joined the staff of the Evening Press, a rank beginner; and of these two employments one lay a matter of four decades back in a half-forgotten past, while the other was of pressing moment, having to do with Major Stone's enjoyment of his daily bread and other elements of nutrition regarded as essential to the sustenance of human life. In his military career he might have been more or less of a success. Certainly he must have acquitted himself with some measure of personal credit; the rank he had attained in the service and the standing he had subsequently enjoyed among his comrades abundantly testified to that.

As a reporter he was absolutely a total loss; for, as already set forth in some detail, he was hopelessly old-fashioned in thought and speech — hopelessly old-fashioned and pedantic in his style of writing; and since his mind mainly concerned itself with retrospections upon the things that happened between April, 1861, and May, 1865, he very naturally — and very frequently — forgot that to a newspaper reporter every day is a new day and a new beginning, and that yesterday always is or always should be ancient history, let alone the time-tarnished yesterdays of forty-odd years ago. Indeed I doubt whether the major ever comprehended that first commandment of the prentice reporter's catechism.

Devore, himself no grand and glittering success as a newspaper man, nevertheless had mighty little use for the pottering, ponderous old major. Devore did not believe that bricks could be made without straw. He considered it a waste of time and raw material to try. Through that summer he kept the major on the payroll solely because the chief so willed it. But, though he might not discharge the major, at least he could bait him — and bait him Devore did — not, mind you, with words, but with a silent, sublimated contempt more bitter and more biting than any words.

So there, on the occasion in question, the situation stood — the major hanging on tooth and nail to his small job, because he needed most desperately the twelve dollars a week it brought him; the city editor regarding him and all his manifold reportorial sins of omission, commission and remission with a corrosive, speechless venom; and the rest of us in the city room divided in our sympathies as between those two. We sympathized with Devore for having to carry so woful an incompetent upon his small and overworked crew; we sympathized with the kindly, gentle, tiresome old major for his bungling, vain attempts to creditably cover the small and piddling assignments that came his way.

I remember the date mighty well — the third of July. For three days now the Democratic party, in national convention assembled at Chicago, had been in the throes of labor. It had been expected — in fact had been as good as promised — that by ten o'clock that evening the deadlock would melt before a sweetly gushing freshet of party harmony and the head of the presidential ticket would be named, wherefore in the Evening Press shop a late shift had stayed on duty to get out an extra. Back in the press-room the press was dressed. A front page form was made up and ready, all but the space where the name of the nominee would be inserted when the flash came; and in the alley outside a picked squad of newsboys, renowned for speed of the leg and carrying quality of the voice, awaited their wares, meanwhile skylarking under the eye of a circulation manager.

Besides, there was no telling when an arrest might be made in the Bullard murder case — that just by itself would provide ample excuse for an extra. Two days had passed and two nights since the killing of Attorney-at-Law Rodney G. Bullard, and still the killing, to quote a favorite line of the local descriptive writers, "remained shrouded in impenetrable mystery." If the police force, now busily engaged in running clues into theories and theories into the ground, should by any blind chance of fortune be lucky enough to ascertain the identity and lay hands upon the person of Bullard's assassin, the whole town, regardless of the hour, would rise up out of bed to read the news of it. It was the biggest crime story that town had known for ten years; one of the biggest crime stories it had ever known.

In the end our waiting all went for nothing. There were no developments at Central Station or elsewhere in the Bullard case, and at Chicago there was no nomination. At nine-thirty a bulletin came over our leased wire saying that Tammany, having been beaten before the Resolutions Committee, was still battling on the floor for its candidate; so that finally the convention had adjourned until morning, and now the delegates were streaming out of the hall, too tired to cheer and almost too tired to jeer — all of which was sad news to us, because it meant that, instead of taking a holiday on the Fourth, we must work until noon at least, and very likely until later. Down that way the Fourth was not observed with quite the firecrackery and skyrockety enthusiasm that marked its celebration in most of the states to the north of us; nevertheless, a day off was a day off and we were deeply disgusted at the turn affairs had taken. It was almost enough to make a fellow feel friendly toward the Republicans.

Following the tension there was a snapback; a feeling of languor and disappointment possessed us. Devore slammed down the lid of his desk and departed, cursing the luck as he went. Harty, the telegraph editor, and Wilbur, the telegraph operator, rolled down their shirtsleeves and, taking their coats over their arms, departed in company for Tony's place up at the corner, where cool beers were to be found and electric fans, and a business men's lunch served at all hours.

That left in the city room four or five men. Sprawled upon battered chairs and draped over battered desks, they inhaled the smells of rancid greases that floated in to them from the back of the building; they coddled their disappointment to keep it warm and they talked shop. When it comes to talking shop in season and out of season, neither stock actors nor hospital surgeons are worse offenders than newspaper reporters — especially young newspaper reporters, as all these men were except only Major Stone.

It was inevitable that the talk should turn upon the Bullard murder, and that the failure of the police force to find the killer or even to find a likely suspect should be the hinge for its turning. For the moment Ike Webb had the floor, expounding his own pet theories. Ike was a good talker — a mighty good reporter too, let me tell you. Across the room from Ike, tilted back in a chair against the wall, sat the major, looking shabby and a bit forlorn. For a month now shabbiness had been seizing on the major, spreading over him like a mildew. It started first with his shoes, which turned brown and then cracked across the toes, it extended to his hat, which sagged in its brim and became a moldy green in its crown, and now it had touched his coat lapels, his waistcoat front, his collar — his rolling Lord Byron collar — and his sleeve ends.

The major's harmlessly pompous manner was all gone from him that night. Of late his self-assurance had seemed to be fraying and frazzling away, along with those old-timey, full-bosomed shirts of which he had in times gone by been so tremendously proud. It was as though the passing of the one marked the passing of the other — symbolic as you might say. Formerly, too, the major had also excelled mightily in miscellaneous conversation, dominating it by sheer weight of tediousness. Now he sat silent while these youngsters with their unthatched lips — born, most of them, after he reached middle age — babbled the jargon of their trade. He considered a little ravelly strip along one of his cuffs solicitously.

Ike Webb was saying this — that the biggest thing in the whole created world was a big scoop — an exclusive, world-beating, bottled-up scoop of a scoop. Nothing that could possibly come into a reporter's life was one-half so big and so glorious and satisfying. He warmed to his theme:

"Gee! fellows, but wouldn't it be great to get a scoop on a thing like this Bullard murder! Just suppose now that one of us, all by himself, found the person who did the shooting and got a full confession from him, whoever he was; and got the gun that it was done with — got the whole thing — and then turned it loose all over the front page before that big stiff of a Chief Gotlieb down at Central Station knew a thing about it. Beating the police to it would be the best part of that job. That's the way they do things in New York. In New York it's the newspapers that do the real work on big murder mysteries, and the police take their tips from them. Why, some of the best detectives in New York are reporters. Look what they did in that Guldensuppe case! Look at what they've done in half a dozen other big cases! Down here we just follow along, like sheep, behind a bunch of fat-necked cops, taking their leavings. Up there a paper turns a man loose, with an unlimited expense account and all the time he needs, and tells him to go to it. That's the right way too!"

By that the others knew Ike Webb was thinking of what Vogel had told him. Vogel was a gifted but admittedly erratic genius from the metropolis who had come upon us as angels sometimes do — unawares — two weeks before, with cinders in his ears and the grime of a dusty right-of-way upon his collar. He had worked for the sheet two weeks and then, on a Saturday night, had borrowed what sums of small change he could and under cover of friendly night had moved on to parts unknown, leaving us dazzled by the careless, somewhat patronizing brilliance of his manner, and stuffed to our earlobes with tales of the splendid, adventurous, bohemian lives that newspaper men in New York lived.

"Well, I know this," put in little Pinky Gilfoil, who was red-headed, red-freckled and red-tempered: "I'd give my right leg to pull off that Bullard story as a scoop. No, not my right leg — a reporter needs all the legs he's got; but I'd give my right arm and throw in an eye for good measure. It would be the making of a reporter in this town — he'd have 'em all eating out of his hand after that." He licked his lips. Even the bare thought of the thing tasted pretty good to Pinky.

"Now you're whistling!" chimed Ike Webb. "The fellow who single-handed got that tale would have a job on this paper as long as he lived. The chief would just naturally have to hand him more money. In New York, though, he'd get a big cash bonus besides, an award they call it up there. I'd go anywhere and do anything and take any kind of a chance to land that story as an exclusive — yes, or any other big story."

To all this the major, it appeared, had been listening, for now he spoke up in a pretty fair imitation of his old impressive manner:

"But, young gentlemen — pardon me — do you seriously think — any of you — that any honorarium, however large, should or could be sufficient temptation to induce one in your — in our profession — to give utterance in print to a matter that he had learned, let us say, in confidence? And suppose also that by printing it he brought suffering or disgrace upon innocent parties. Unless one felt that he was serving the best ends of society — unless one, in short, were actuated by the highest of human motives — could one afford to do such a thing? And, under any circumstances, could one violate a trust — could one violate the common obligation of a gentleman's rules of deportment —"

"Major," broke in Ike Webb earnestly, "the way I look at it, a reporter can't afford too many of the luxuries you're mentioning. His duty, it seems to me, is to his paper first and the rest of the world afterward. His paper ought to be his mother and his father and all his family. If he gets a big scoop — no matter how he gets it or where he gets it — he ought to be able to figure out some way of getting it into print. It's not alone what he owes his paper — it's what he owes himself. Personally I wouldn't be interested for a minute in bringing the person that killed Rod Bullard to justice — that's not the point. He was a pretty shady person — Rod Bullard. By all accounts he got what was coming to him. It's the story itself that I'd want."

"Say, listen here, major," put in Pinky Gilfoil, suddenly possessed of a strengthening argument; "I reckon back yonder in the Civil War, when you all got the smoke of battle in your noses, you didn't stop to consider that you were about to make a large crop of widows and orphans and cause suffering to a whole slue of innocent people that'd never done you any harm! You didn't stop then, did you? I'll bet you didn't — you just sailed in! It was your duty — the right thing to do — and you just went and did it. 'War is hell!' Sherman said. Well, so is newspaper work hell — in a way. And smelling out a big story ought to be the same to a reporter that the smoke of battle is to a soldier. That's right — I'll leave it to any fellow here if that ain't right!" he wound up, forgetting in his enthusiasm to be grammatical.

It was an unfortunate simile to be making and Pinky should have known better, for at Pinky's last words the old major's mild eye widened and, expanding himself, he brought his chair legs down to the floor with a thump.

"Ah, yes!" he said, and his voice took on still more of its old ringing quality. "Speaking of battles, I am just reminded, young gentlemen, that tomorrow is the anniversary of the fall of Vicksburg. Though Northern-born, General Pemberton was a gallant officer — none of our own Southern leaders was more gallant — but it has always seemed to me that his defense of Vicksburg was marked by a series of the most lamentable and disastrous mistakes. If you care to listen, I will explain further." And he squared himself forward, with one short, plump hand raised, ready to tick off his points against Pemberton upon his fingers.

By experience dearly bought at the expense of our ear-drums, the members of the Evening Press staff knew what that meant; for as you already know, the major's conversational specialty was the Civil War — it and its campaigns. Describing it, he made even war a commonplace and a tiresome topic. In his hands an account of the hardest fought battle became a tremendously uninteresting thing. He weeded out all the thrills and in their places planted hedges of dusty, deadly dry statistics. When the major started on the war it was time to be going.

One by one the youngsters got up and slipped out. Presently the major, booming away like a bell buoy, became aware that his audience had dwindled. Only Ike Webb remained, and Ike was getting upon his feet and reaching for the peg where his coat swung.

"I'm sorry to leave you right in the middle of your story, major; but, honestly, I've got to be going," apologized Ike. "Good night, and don't forget this, major" — Ike had halted at the door — "when a big story comes your way freeze to it with both hands and slam it across the plate as a scoop. Do that and you can give 'em all the laugh. Good night again — see you in the morning, major!"

He grinned to himself as he turned away. The major was a mighty decent, tender-hearted little old scout, a gentleman by birth and breeding, even if he was down and out and dog-poor. It was a shame that Devore kept him skittering round on little picayunish jobs — running errands, that was really what it was. Still, at that, the old major was no reporter and never would be. He wouldn't know a big story if he ran into it on the big road — it would have to burst right in his face before he recognized it. And even then the chances were that he wouldn't know what to do with it. It was enough to make a fellow grin.

Deserted by the last of his youthful compatriots — which was what he himself generally called them — the major lingered a moment in heavy thought. He glanced about the cluttered city room, now suddenly grown large and empty. This was the theater where his own little drama of unfitness and failure and private mortification had been staged and acted. It had run nearly a month now, and a month is a long run for a small tragedy in a newspaper office or anywhere else. He shook his head. He shook it as though he were trying to shake it clear of a job lot of old-fashioned, antiquated ideals — as though he were trying to make room for newer, more useful, more modern conceptions. Then he settled his aged and infirm slouch hat more firmly upon his round-domed skull, straightened his shoulders and stumped out.

At the second turning up the street from the office an observant onlooker might have noticed a small, an almost imperceptible change in the old man's bearing. There was not a sneaky bone in the major's body — he walked as he thought and as he talked, in straight lines; but before he turned the corner he glanced up and down the empty sidewalk in a quick, furtive fashion, and after he had swung into the side street a trifle of the steam seemed gone from his stiff-spined, hard-heeled gait. It ceased to be a strut; it became a plod.

The street he had now entered was a badly lighted street, with long stretches of murkiness between small patches of gas-lamped brilliance. By day the houses that walled it would have showed themselves as shabby and gone to seed — the sort of houses that second cousins move into after first families have moved out. Two-thirds of the way along the block the major turned in at a sagged gate. He traversed a short walk of seamed and decrepit flagging, where tufts of rank grass sprouted between the fractures in the limestone slabs, and mounted the front porch of a house that had cheap boarding house written all over it.

When the major opened the front door the tepid smell that gushed out to greet him was the smell of a cheap boarding house too, if you know what I mean — a spilt-kerosene, boiled-cabbage, dust-in-the-corners smell. Once upon a time the oilcloth upon the floor of the entry way had exhibited a vivid and violent pattern of green octagons upon a red and yellow background, but that had been in some far distant day of its youth and freshness. Now it was worn to a scaly, crumbly color of nothing at all, and it was frayed into fringes at the door and in places scuffed clear through, so that the knot-holes of the naked planking showed like staring eyes.

Standing just inside the hall, the major glanced down first at the floor and then up to where in a pendent nub a pinprick of light like a captive lightning-bug flickered up and down feebly as the air pumped through the pipe; and out of his chest the major fetched a small sigh. It was a sigh of resignation, but it had loneliness in it too. Well, it was a come-down, after all these peaceful and congenial years spent among the marble-columned, red-plushed glories of the old Gaunt House, to be living in this place.

The major had been here now almost a month. Very quietly, almost secretly, he had come hither when he found that by no amount of stretching could his pay as a reporter on the Evening Press be made to cover the cost of living as he had been accustomed to live prior to that disastrous day when the major waked up in the morning to find that all his inherited investments had vanished over night — and, vanishing so, had taken with them the small but sufficient income that had always been ample for his needs.

In that month the major had seen but one or two of his fellow lodgers, slouching forms that passed him by in the gloom of the half-lighted hallways or on the creaky stairs. His landlady he saw but once a week — on Saturday, which was settlement day. She was a forlorn, gray creature, half blind, and she felt her way about gropingly. By the droop in her spine and by the corners of her lips, permanently puckered from holding pins in her mouth, a close observer would have guessed that she had been a seamstress before her eyes gave out on her and she took to keeping lodgers. Of the character of the establishment the innocent old major knew nothing; he knew that it was cheap and that it was on a quiet by-street, and for his purposes that was sufficient.

He heaved another small sigh and passed slowly up the worn steps of the stairwell until he came to the top of the house. His room was on the attic floor, the middle room of the three that lined the bare hall on one side. The door-knob was broken off; only its iron center remained. His fingers slipped as he fumbled for a purchase upon the metal core; but finally, after two attempts, he gripped it and it turned, admitting him into the darkness of a stuffy interior. The major made haste to open the one small window before he lit the single gas jet. Its guttery flare exposed a bed, with a thin mattress and a skimpy cover, shoved close up under the sloping wall; a sprained chair on its last legs; an old horsehide trunk; a shaky washstand of cheap yellow pine, garnished forth with an ewer and a basin; a limp, frayed towel; and a minute segment of pale pink soap.

Major Stone was in the act of removing his coat when he became aware of a certain sound, occurring at quick intervals. In the posture of a plump and mature robin he cocked his head on one side to listen; and now he remembered that he had heard the same sound the night before, and the night before that. These times, though, he had heard it intermittently and dimly, as he tossed about half awake and half asleep, trying to accommodate his elderly bones to the irregularities of his hot and uncomfortable bed. But now he heard it more plainly, and at once he recognized it for what it was — the sound of a woman crying; a wrenching succession of deep, racking gulps, and in between them little moaning, panting breaths, as of utter exhaustion — a sound such as might be distilled from the very dregs of a grief too great to be borne.

He looked about him, his eyes and ears searching for further explanation of this. He had it. There was a door set in the cross-wall of his room — a door bolted and nailed up. It had a transom over it and against the dirty glass of the transom a light was reflected, and through the door and the transom the sound came. The person in trouble, whoever it might be, was in that next room — and that person was a woman and she was in dire distress. There was a compelling note in her sobbing.

Undecided, Major Stone stood a minute rubbing his nose pensively with a small forefinger; then the resolution to act fastened upon him. He slipped his coat back on, smoothed down his thin mane of reddish gray hair with his hands, stepped out into the hall and rapped delicately with a knuckled finger upon the door of the next room. There was no answer, so he rapped a little harder; and at that a sob checked itself and broke off chokingly in the throat that uttered it. From within a voice came. It was a shaken, tear-drained voice — flat and uncultivated.

"Who's there?" The major cleared his throat. "Is it a woman — or a man?" demanded the unseen speaker without waiting for an answer to the first question.

"It is a gentleman," began the major — "a gentleman who —"

"Come on in!" she bade him — "the door ain't latched."

And at that the major turned the knob and looked into a room that was practically a counterpart of his own, except that, instead of a trunk, a cheap imitation-leather suitcase stood upright on the floor, its sides bulging and strained from over-packing. Upon the bed, fully dressed, was stretched a woman — or, rather, a girl. Her head was just rising from the crumpled pillow and her eyes, red-rimmed and widely distended, stared full into his.

What she saw, as she sat up, was a short, elderly man with a solicitous, gentle face; the coat sleeves were turned back off his wrists and his linen shirt jutted out between the unfastened upper buttons and buttonholes of his waistcoat. What the major saw was a girl of perhaps twenty or maybe twenty-two — in her present state it was hard to guess — with hunched-in shoulders and dyed, stringy hair falling in a streaky disarray down over her face like unraveled hemp.

It was her face that told her story. Upon the drawn cheeks and the drooped, woful lips there was no dabbing of cosmetics now; the professional smile, painted, pitiable and betraying, was lacking from the characterless mouth, yet the major — sweet-minded, clean-living old man though he was — knew at a glance what manner of woman he had found here in this lodging house. It was the face of a woman who never intentionally does any evil and yet rarely gets a chance to do any good — a weak, indecisive, commonplace face; and every line in it was a line of least resistance.

That then was what these two saw in each other as they stared a moment across the intervening space. It was the girl who took the initiative.

"Are you one of the police?" Then instantly on the heels of the query: "No; I know better'n that — you ain't no police!"

Her voice was unmusical, vulgar and husky from much weeping. Magically, though, she had checked her sobbing to an occasional hard gulp that clicked down in her throat.

"No, ma'am," said Major Stone, with a grave and respectful courtesy, "I am not connected with the police department. I am a professional man — associated at this time with the practice of journalism. I have the apartment or chamber adjoining yours and, accidentally overhearing a member of the opposite sex in seeming distress, I took it upon myself to offer any assistance that might lie within my power. If I am intruding I will withdraw."

"No," she said; "it ain't no intrusion. I wisht, please, sir, you'd come in jest a minute anyway. I feel like I jest got to talk to somebody a minute. I'm sorry, though, if I disturbed you by my cryin' — but I jest couldn't help it. Last night and the night before — that was the first night I come here — I cried all night purty near; but I kept my head in the bedclothes. But tonight, after it got dark up here and me layin' here all alone, I felt 's if I couldn't stand it no longer.

Honest, I like to died! Right this minute I'm almost plum' distracted."

The major advanced a step.

"I assure you I deeply regret to learn of your unhappiness," he said. "If you desire it I will be only too glad to summon our worthy landlady, Miss — Miss —" he paused.

"Miss La Mode," she said, divining — "Blanche La Mode — that's my name. I come from Indianapolis, Indiana. But please, mister, don't call that there woman. I don't want to see her. For a while I didn't think I wanted to see nobody, and yit I've known all along, from the very first, that sooner or later I'd jest naturally have to talk to somebody. I knew I'd jest have to!" she repeated with a kind of weak intensity. "And it might jest as well be you as anybody, I guess."

She sat up on the side of the bed, dangling her feet, and subconsciously the major took in fuller details of her attire — the cheap white slippers with rickety, worn-down high heels; the sleazy stockings; the over-decorated skirt of shabby blue cloth; the soiled and rumpled waist of coarse lace, gaping away from the scrawny neck, where the fastenings had pulled awry. Looped about her throat and dangling down on her flat breast, where they heaved up and down with her breathing, was a double string of pearls that would have been worth ten thousand dollars had they been genuine pearls. A hand which was big-knuckled and thin held a small, moist wad of handkerchief. About her there was something unmistakably bucolic, and yet she was town-branded, too, flesh and soul. Major Stone bowed with the ceremonious detail that was a part of him.

"My name, ma'am, is Stone — Major Putnam Stone, at your service," he told her.

"Yes, sir," she said, seeming not to catch either his name or his title. "Well, mister, I'm goin' to tell you something that'll maybe surprise you. I ain't goin' to ast you not to tell anybody, 'cause I guess you will anyhow, sooner or later; and it don't make much difference if you do. But seems's if I can't hold in no longer. I guess maybe I'll feel easier in my own mind when I git it all told. Shet that door — jest close it — the lock is broke — and set down in that chair, please, sir."

The major closed the latchless door and took the one tottery chair. The girl remained where she was, on the side of her bed, her slippered feet dangling, her eyes fixed on a spot where there was a three-cornered break in the dirty-gray plastering.

"You know about Rodney G. Bullard, the lawyer, don't you? — about him bein' found shot day before yistiddy evenin' in the mouth of that alley?" she asked.

"Yes, ma'am," he said. "Though I was not personally acquainted with the man himself, I am familiar with the circumstances you mention."

"Well," she said, with a sort of jerk behind each word, "it was me that done it!"

"I beg your pardon," he said, half doubting whether he had heard aright, "but what was it you said you did?"

"Shot him!" she answered — "I was the one that shot him — with this thing here." She reached one hand under the pillow and drew out a short-barreled, stubby revolver and extended it to him. Mechanically he took it, and thereafter for a space he held it in his hands. The girl went straight on, pouring out her sentences with a driven, desperate eagerness.

"I didn't mean to do it, though — God knows I didn't mean to do it! He treated me mighty sorry — it was lowdown and mean all the way through, the way he done me — but I didn't mean him no real harm. I was only aimin' to skeer him into doin' the right thing by me. It was accidental-like — it really was, mister! In all my life I ain't never intentionally done nobody any harm. And yit it seems like somebody's forever and a day imposin' on me!" She quavered with the puny passion of her protest against the world that had bruised and beaten her as with rods.

Shocked, stunned, the major sat in a daze, making little clucking sounds in his throat. For once in his conversational life he couldn't think of the right words to say. He fumbled the short pistol in his hands.

"I'm goin' to tell you the whole story, jest like it was," she went on in her flat drone; and the words she spoke seemed to come to him from a long way off. "That there Rodney Bullard he tricked me somethin' shameful. He come to the town where I was livin' to make a speech in a political race, and we got acquainted and he made up to me. I was workin' in a hotel there — one of the dinin' room help. That was two years ago this comin' September. Well, the next day, when he left, he got me to come 'long with him. He said he'd look after me. I liked him some then and he talked mighty big about what he was goin' to do for me; so I come with him. He told me that I could be his —" She hesitated.

"His amanuensis, perhaps," suggested the old man.

"Which?" she said. "No; it wasn't that way — he didn't say nothin' about marryin' me and I didn't expect him to. He told me that I should be his girl — that was all; but he didn't keep his word — no, sir; right from the very first he broke his word to me! It wasn't more'n a month after I got here before he quit comin' to see me at all. Well, after that I stayed a spell longer at the house where I was livin' and then I went to another house — Vic Magner's. You know who she is, I reckin?"

The major half nodded, half shook his head.

"By reputation only I know the person in question," he answered a bit stiffly.

"Well," she went on, "there ain't so much more to tell. I've been sick lately — I had a right hard spell. I ain't got my strength all back yit. I was laid up three weeks, and last Monday, when I was up and jest barely able to crawl round,

Vic Magner, she come to me and told me that I'd have to git out unless I could git somebody to stand good for my board. I owed her for three weeks already and I didn't have but nine dollars to my name. I offered her that, but she said she wanted it all or nothin'. I think she wanted to git shet of me anyway. Mister, I was mighty weak and discouraged — I was so! I didn't know what to do.

"I hadn't seen Rod Bullard for goin' on more than a year, but he was the only one I could think of; so I slipped out of the house and went acrost the street to a grocery store where there was a pay station, and I called him up on the telephone and ast him to help me out a little. It wasn't no more than right that he should, was it, seein' as he was responsible for my comin' here? Besides, if it hadn't been for him in the first place I wouldn't never 'a' got into all that trouble. I talked with him over the telephone at his office and he said he'd do somethin' for me. He said he'd send me some money that evenin' or else he'd bring it round himself. But he didn't do neither one. And Vic Magner, she kept on doggin' after me for her board money.

"I telephoned him again the next mornin'; but before I could say more'n two words to him he got mad and told me to quit botherin' him, and he rung off. That was day before yistiddy. When I got back to the house Vic Magner come to me, and I couldn't give her no satisfaction. So about six o'clock in the evenin' she made me pack up and git out. I didn't have nowheres to go and only eight dollars and ninety cents left — I'd spent a dime telephoning so, before I got out I took and wrote Rod Bullard a note, and when I got outside I give a little nigger boy fifteen cents to take it to him. I told him in the note I was out in the street, without nowheres to go, and that if he didn't meet me that night and do somethin' for me I'd jest have to come to his office. I said for him to meet me at eight o'clock at the mouth of Grayson Street Alley. That give me two hours to wait. I walked round and round, packin' my baggage.

"Then I come by a pawnstore and seen a lot of pistols in the window, and I went in and I bought one for two dollars and a half. The pawnstore man he throwed in the shells. But I wasn't aimin' to hurt Rod Bullard — jest to skeer him. I was thinkin' some of killin' myself too. Then I walked round some more till I was plum' wore out.

"When eight o'clock come I was waitin' where I said, and purty soon he come along. As soon as he saw me standin' there in the shadder he bulged up to me. He was mighty mad. He called me out of my name and said I didn't have no claims on him — a whole lot more like that — and said he didn't purpose to be bothered with me phonin' him and writin' him notes and callin' on him for money. I said somethin' back, and then he made like he was goin' to hit me with his fist. I'd had that pistol in my hand all the time, holdin' it behind my skirt. And I pulled it and I pointed it like I was goin' to shoot — jest to skeer him, though, and make him do the right thing by me. I jest simply pointed it at him — that's all. I didn't have no idea it would go off without you pulled the hammer back first!

"Then it happened! It went off right in my hand. And he said to me: 'Now you've done it!' — jest like that. He walked away from me about ten feet, and started to lean up against a tree, and then he fell down right smack on his face. And I grabbed up my baggage and run away. I wasn't sorry about him. I ain't been sorry about him a minute since — ain't that funny? But I was awful skeered!"

Rocking her body back and forth from the hips, she put her hands up to her face. Major Stone stared at her, his mind in a twisting eddy of confused thoughts. Perhaps it was the clearest possible betrayal of his utter unfitness for his new vocation in life that not until that very moment when the girl had halted her narrative did it come to him — and it came then with a sudden jolt — that here he had one of those monumental news stories for which young Gilfoil or young Webb would be willing to barter his right arm and throw in an eye for good measure. It was a scoop, as those young fellows had called it — an exclusive confession of a big crime — a thing that would mean much to any paper and to any reporter who brought it to his paper. It would transform a failure into a conspicuous success. It would put more money into a pay envelope. And he had it all! Sheer luck had brought it to him and flung it into his lap.

Nor was he under any actual pledge of secrecy. This girl had told it to him freely, of her own volition. It was not in the nature of her to keep her secret. She had told it to him, a stranger; she would tell it to other strangers — or else somebody would betray her. And surely this sickly, slack-twisted little wanton would be better off inside the strong arm of the law than outside it? No jury of Southern men would convict her of murder — the thought was incredible. She would be kindly dealt with. In one illuminating flash the major divined that these would have been the inevitable conclusions of any one of those ambitious young men at the office. He bent forward.

"What did you do then, ma'am?" he asked.

"I didn't know what to do," she said, dropping her hands into her lap. "I run till I couldn't run no more, and then I walked and walked and walked. I reckin I must 'a' walked ten miles. And then, when I was jest about to drop, I come past this house. There was a light burnin' on the porch and I could make out to read the sign on the door, and it said Lodgers Taken.

"So I walked in and rung the bell, and when the woman came I said I'd jest got here from the country and wanted a room. She charged me two dollars a week, in advance; and I paid her two dollars down — and she showed me the way up here.

"I've been here ever since, except twice when I slipped out to buy me somethin' to eat at a grocery store and to git some newspapers. At first I figgered the police would be a-comin' after me; but they didn't — there wasn't nobody at all seen the shootin', I reckin. And I was skeered Vic Magner might tell on me; but I guess she didn't want to run no risk of gittin' in trouble herself — that Captain Brennan, of the Second Precinct, he's been threatenin' to run her out of town the first good chance he got. And there wasn't none of the other girls there that knowed I ever knew Rod Bullard. So, you see, I ain't been arrested yit.

"Layin' here yistiddy all day, with nothin' to do but think and cry, I made up my mind I'd kill myself. I tried to do it. I took that there pistol out and I put it up to my head and I said to myself that all I had to do was jest to pull on that trigger thing and it wouldn't hurt me but a secont — and maybe not that long. But I couldn't do it, mister — I jest couldn't do it at all. It seemed like I wanted to die, and yit I wanted to live too. All my life I've been jest that way — first thinkin' about doin' one thing and then another, and hardly ever doin' either one of 'em.

"Here on this bed tonight I got to thinkin' if I could jest tell somebody about it that maybe after that I'd feel easier in my mind. And right that very minute you come and knocked on the door, and I knowed it was a sign — I knowed you was the one for me to tell it to. And so I've done it, and already I think I feel a little bit easier in my mind. And so that's all, mister. But I wisht please you'd take that pistol away with you when you go — I don't never want to see it again as long as I live."

She paused, huddling herself in a heap upon the bed. The major's short arm made a gesture toward the cheap suitcase.

"I observe," he said, "that your portmanteau is packed as if for a journey. Were you thinking of leaving, may I ask?"

"My which?" she said. "Oh, you mean my baggage! Yes; I ain't never unpacked it since I come here. I was aimin' to go back to my home — I got a stepsister livin' there and she might take me in — only after payin' for this room I ain't got quite enough money to take me there; and now I don't know as I want to go, either. If I kin git my strength back I might stay on here — I kind of like city life. Or I might go up to Cincinnati. A girl that I used to know here is livin' there now and she wrote to me a couple of times, and I know her address — it was backed on the envelope. Still, I ain't sure — my plans ain't all made yit. Sometimes I think I'll give myself up, but most generally I think I won't. I've got to do somethin' purty soon though, one way or another, because I ain't got but a little over three dollars left out of what I had."

She sank her head in the pillow wearily, with her face turned away from him. The major stood up. Into his side coat pocket he slipped the revolver that had snuffed out the late and unsavory Rodney Bullard's light of life, and from his trousers pocket he slowly drew forth his supply of ready money. He had three silver dollars, one quarter, one dime, and a nickel — three-forty in all. Contemplating the disks of metal in the palm of his hand, he did a quick sum in mental arithmetic. This was Thursday night now. Saturday afternoon at two he would draw a pay envelope containing twelve dollars. Meantime he must eat. Well, if he stinted himself closely a dollar might be stretched to bridge the gap until Saturday. The major had learned a good deal about the noble art of stinting these last few weeks.

On the coverlet alongside the girl he softly piled two of the silver dollars and the forty cents in change. Then, after a momentary hesitation, he put down the third silver dollar, gathered up the forty cents, slid it gently into his pocket and started for the door, the loose planks creaking under his tread. At the threshold he halted.

"Good night, Miss La Mode," he said. "I trust your night's repose may be restful and refreshing to you, ma'am."

She lifted her face from the pillow and spoke, without turning to look at him.

"Mister," she said, "I've told you the whole truth about that thing and I ain't goin' to lie to you about anythin' else. I didn't come from Indianapolis, Indiana, like I told you. My home is in Swainboro', this state — a little town. You might know where it is? And my real name ain't La Mode, neither. I taken it out of a book — the La Mode part — and I always did think Blanche was an awful sweet name for a girl. But my real name is Gussie Stammer. Good night, mister. I'm much obliged to you fer listenin', and I ain't goin' to disturb you no more with my cryin' if I kin help it."

As the major gently closed her door behind him he heard her give a long, sleepy sigh, like a tired child. Back in his own room he glanced about him, meanwhile feeling himself over for writing material. He found in his pockets a pencil and a couple of old letters, whereas he knew he needed a big sheaf of copy paper for the story he had to write. Anyway, there was no place here to do an extended piece of writing — no desk and no comfortable chair. The office would be a much better place.

The office was only a matter of two or three blocks away. The negro watchman would be there; he stayed on duty all night. Using the corner of his washstand for a desk, the major set down his notes — names, places, details, dates — upon the backs of his two letters. This done, he settled his ancient hat on his head, picked up his cane, and in another minute was tiptoeing down the stairs and out the front doorway. Once outside, his tread took on the brisk emphasis of one set upon an important task and in a hurry to do it.

Ten minutes later Major Stone sat at his desk in the empty city room of the Evening Press. Except for Henry, the old black night watchman, there was no other person in the building anywhere. Just over his head an incandescent bulb blazed, bringing out in strong relief the major's intent old face, mullioned with crisscross lines. A cedar pencil, newly sharpened, was in his fingers; under his right hand was a block of clean copy paper. His notes lay in front of him, the little stubnosed pistol serving as a paper weight to hold the two wrinkled envelopes flat. Through the loop of the trigger guard the words, Gussie Stammer, alias Blanche La Mode, showed. Everything was ready.

The major hesitated, though. He readjusted his paper and fidgeted his pencil. He scratched his head and pulled at the little tuft of goatee under his lower lip. Like many a more experienced author, Major Stone was having trouble getting under way. He had his own ideas about a fitting introductory paragraph. Coming along, he had thought up a full sonorous one, with a biblical injunction touching on the wages of sin embodied in it; but, on the other hand, there was to be borne in mind the daily-dinned injunction of Devore that every important news item should begin with a sentence in which the whole story was summed up. Finally Major Stone made a beginning. He covered nearly a sheet of paper.

Then, becoming suddenly dissatisfied with it, he tore up what he had written and started all over again, only to repeat the same operation. Two salty drops rolled down his face and fell upon the paper, and instantly little twin blistered blobs like tearmarks appeared on its clear surface. They were not tears, though — they were drops of sweat wrung from the major's brow by the pains of creation. Again he poised his pencil and again he halted it in the air — he needed inspiration. His gaze rested absently upon the pistol; absently he picked it up and began examining it.

It was a cheap, rusted, second-hand thing, poorly made, but no doubt deadly enough at close range. He unbreeched it and spun the cylinder with his thumb and spilled the contents into his palm — four loaded shells, suety and slick with grease, and one that had been recently fired; and it was discolored and flattened a trifle. Each of the four loaded shells had a small cap like a little round staring eye set in the exact center of its flanged butt-end, but the eye of the fifth shell was punched in. He turned the empty weapon in his hands, steadying its mechanism, and as he did so a scent of burnt powder, stale and dead, came to him out of the fouled muzzle. He wrinkled his nose and sniffed at it.

It had been many a long day since the major had had that smell in his nostrils — many a long, long day. But there had been a time when it was familiar enough to him. Even now it brought the clamoring memories of that far distant time back to him, fresh and vivid. It stimulated his imagination, quickening his mind with big thoughts. It recalled those four years when he had fought for a principle, and had kept on fighting even when the substance of the thing he fought for was gone and there remained but the empty husks. It recalled those last few hopeless months when the forlorn hope had become indeed a lost cause; when the forty cents he now carried in his pocket would have seemed a fortune; when the sorry house where he lodged now would have seemed a palace; when, without prospect or hope of reward or victory, he had piled risk upon risk, had piled sacrifice upon sacrifice, and through it all had borne it all without whimper or complaint — fighting the good fight like a soldier, keeping the faith like a gentleman. It was the Smoke of Battle!

The major had his inspiration now, right enough. He knew just what he would write; knew just how he would write it. He laid down the pistol and the shells and squared off and straightway began writing. For two hours nearly he wrote away steadily, rarely changing or erasing a word, stopping only to repoint the lead of his pencil. Methodically as a machine he covered sheet after sheet with his fine old-fashioned script. Never for one instant did he hesitate or falter.

Just before one o'clock he finished. The completed manuscript, each page of the twenty-odd pages properly numbered, lay in a neat pile before him. He scooped up the pistol shells and stored them in an inner breast pocket of his coat; then he opened a drawer, slipped the emptied revolver well back under a riffle of papers and clippings and closed the drawer and locked it. His notes he tore into squares, and those squares into smaller squares — and so on until the fragments would tear no finer, but fluttered out between his fingers in a small white shower like stage snow.

He shoved his completed narrative back under the roll-top of Devore's desk, where the city editor would see it the very first thing when he came to work; and as he straightened up with a little grunt of satisfaction and stretched his arms out the last of his fine-linen shirts, with a rending sound, ripped down the plaited front, from collarband almost to waistline.

He eyed the ruined bosom with a regretful stare, plucking at the gaping tear with his graphite-dusted fingers and shaking his head mournfully. Yet as he stepped out into the street, bound for his lodgings, he jarred his heels down upon the sidewalk with the brisk, snapping gait of a man who has tackled a hard job and has done it well, and is satisfied with the way he has done it.

Under a large black head the major's story was printed in the Fourth of July edition of the Evening Press. It ran full two columns and lapped over into a third column. It was an exhaustive — and exhausting — account of the Fall of Vicksburg.

VI

THE EXIT OF ANSE
DUGMORE

When a Kentucky mountaineer goes to the penitentiary the chances are that he gets sore eyes from the white walls that enclose him, or quick consumption from the thick air that he breathes. It was entirely in accordance with the run of his luck that Anse Dugmore should get them both, the sore eyes first and then the consumption.

There is seldom anything that is picturesque about the man-killer of the mountain country. He is lacking sadly in the romantic aspect and the delightfully studied vernacular with which an inspired school of fiction has invested our Western gun-fighter. No alluring jingle of belted accouterment goes with him, no gift of deadly humor adorns his equally deadly gun-play. He does his killing in an unemotional, unattractive kind of way, with absolutely no regard for costume or setting. Rarely is he a fine figure of a man.

Take Anse Dugmore now. He had a short-waisted, thin body and abnormally long, thin legs, like the shadow a man casts at sunup. He didn't have that steel-gray eye of which we so often read. His eyes weren't of any particular color, and he had a straggly mustache of sandy red and no chin worth mentioning; but he could shoot off a squirrel's head, or a man's, at the distance of a considerable number of yards.

Until he was past thirty he played merely an incidental part in the tribal war that had raged up and down Yellow Banks Creek and its principal tributary, the Pigeon Roost, since long before the Big War. He was getting out timber to be floated down the river on the spring rise when word came to him of an ambuscade that made him the head of his immediate clan and the upholder of his family's honor.

"Yore paw an' yore two brothers was laywaid this mawnin' comin' 'long Yaller Banks togither," was the message brought by a breathless bearer of news. "The wimmenfolks air totin' 'em home now. Talt, he ain't dead yit."

From a dry spot behind a log Anse lifted his rifle and started over the ridge with the long, shambling gait of the born hill-climber that eats up the miles. For this emergency he had been schooled years back when he sat by a wood fire in a cabin of split boards and listened to his crippled-up father reciting the saga of the feud, with the tally of this one killed and that one maimed; for this he had been schooled when he practised with rifle and revolver until, even as a boy, his aim had become as near an infallible thing as anything human gets to be; for this he had been schooled still more when he rode, armed and watchful, to church or court or election. Its coming found him ready.

Two days he ranged the ridges, watching his chance. The Tranthams were hard to find. They were barricaded in their log-walled strongholds, well guarded in anticipation of expected reprisals, and prepared in due season to come forth and prove by a dozen witnesses, or two dozen if so many should be needed to establish the alibi, that they had no hand in the massacre of the Dugmores.

But two days and nights of still-hunting, of patiently lying in wait behind brush fences, of noiseless, pussy-footed patrolling in likely places, brought the survivor of the decimated Dugmores his chance. He caught Pegleg Trantham riding down Red Bird Creek on a mare-mule. Pegleg was only a distant connection of the main strain of the enemy. It was probable that he had no part in the latest murdering; perhaps doubtful that he had any prior knowledge of the plot. But by his name and his blood-tie he was a Trantham, which was enough.

A writer of the Western school would have found little in this encounter that was really worth while to write about. Above the place of the meeting rose the flank of the mountain, scarred with washes and scantily clothed with stunted trees, so that in patches the soil showed through like the hide of a mangy hound. The creek was swollen by the April rains and ran bank-full through raw, red walls. Old Pegleg came cantering along with his rifle balanced on the sliding withers of his mare-mule, for he rode without a saddle. He was an oldish man and fat for a mountaineer. A ten-year-old nephew rode behind him, with his short arms encircling his uncle's paunch. The old man wore a dirty white shirt with a tabbed bosom; a single shiny white china button held the neckband together at the back. Below the button the shirt billowed open, showing his naked back. His wooden leg stuck straight out to the side, its worn brass tip carrying a blob of red mud, and his good leg dangled down straight, with the trousers hitched half-way up the bare shank and a soiled white-yarn sock falling down into the wrinkled and gaping top of an ancient congress gaiter.

From out of the woods came Anse Dugmore, bareheaded, crusted to his knees with dried mud and wet from the rain that had been dripping down since daybreak. A purpose showed in all the lines of his slouchy frame.

Pegleg jerked his rifle up, but he was hampered by the boy's arms about his middle and by his insecure perch upon the peaks of the slab-sided mule. The man afoot fired before the mounted enemy could swing his gunbarrel into line. The bullet ripped away the lower part of Pegleg's face and grazed the cheek of the crouching youngster behind him. The white-eyed nephew slid head first off the buck-jumping mule and instantly scuttled on all fours into the underbrush. The rifle dropped out of Trantham's hands and he lurched forward on the mule's neck, grabbing out with blind, groping motions. Dugmore stepped two paces forward to free his eyes of the smoke, which eddied back from his gunmuzzle into his face, and fired twice rapidly. The mule was bouncing up and down, sideways, in a mild panic. Pegleg rolled off her, as inert as a sack of grits, and lay face upward in the path, with his arms wide outspread on the mud. The mule galloped off in a restrained and dignified style until she was a hundred yards away, and then, having snorted the smells of burnt powder and fresh blood out of her nostrils, she fell to cropping the young leaves off the wayside bushes, mouthing the tender green shoots on her heavy iron bit contentedly.

For a long minute Anse Dugmore stood in the narrow footpath, listening. Then he slid three new shells into his rifle, and slipping down the bank he crossed the creek on a jam of driftwood and, avoiding the roads that followed the little watercourse, made over the shoulder of the mountain for his cabin, two miles down on the opposite side. When he was gone from sight the nephew of the dead Trantham rolled out of his hiding place and fled up the road, holding one hand to his wounded cheek and whimpering. Presently a gaunt, half-wild boar pig, with his spine arched like the mountains, came sniffing slowly down the hill, pausing frequently to cock his wedge-shaped head aloft and fix a hostile eye on two turkey buzzards that began to swing in narrowing circles over one particular spot on the bank of the creek.

The following day Anse sent word to the sheriff that he would be coming in to give himself up. It would not have been etiquette for the sheriff to come for him. He came in, well guarded on the way by certain of his clan, pleaded self-defense before a friendly county judge and was locked up in a one-cell log jail. His own cousin was the jailer and ministered to him kindly. He avoided passing the single barred window of the jail in the daytime or at night when there was a light behind him, and he expected to "come clear" shortly, as was customary.

But the Tranthams broke the rules of the game. The circuit judge lived half-way across the mountains in a county on the Virginia line; he was not an active partizan of either side in the feud. These Tranthams, disregarding all the ethics, went before this circuit judge and asked him for a change of venue, and got it, which was more; so that instead of being tried in Clayton County — and promptly acquitted — Anse Dugmore was taken to Woodbine County and there lodged in a shiny new brick jail. Things were in process of change in Woodbine. A spur of the railroad had nosed its way up from the lowlands and on through the Gap, and had made Loudon, the county-seat, a division terminal. Strangers from the North had come in, opening up the mountains to mines and sawmills and bringing with them many swarthy foreign laborers. A young man of large hopes and an Eastern college education had started a weekly newspaper and was talking big, in his editorial columns, of a new order of things. The foundation had even been laid for a graded school. Plainly Woodbine County was falling out of touch with the century-old traditions of her sisters to the north and west of her.

In due season, then, Anse Dugmore was brought up on a charge of homicide. The trial lasted less than a day. A jury of strangers heard the stories of Anse himself and of the dead Pegleg's white-eyed nephew. In the early afternoon they came back, a wooden toothpick in each mouth, from the new hotel where they had just had a most satisfying fifty-cent dinner at the expense of the commonwealth, and sentenced the defendant, Anderson Dugmore, to state prison at hard labor for the balance of his natural life.

The sheriff of Woodbine padlocked on Anse's ankles a set of leg irons that had been made by a mountain blacksmith out of log chains and led him to the new depot. It was Anse Dugmore's first ride on a railroad train; also it was the first ride on any train for Wyatt Trantham, head of the other clan, who, having been elected to the legislature while Anse lay in jail, had come over from Clayton, bound for the state capital, to draw his mileage and be a statesman.

It was not in the breed for the victorious Trantham to taunt his hobbled enemy or even to look his way, but he sat just across the aisle from the prisoner so that his ear might catch the jangle of the heavy irons when Dugmore moved in his seat. They all left the train together at the little blue-painted Frankfort station, Trantham turning off at the first crossroads to go where the round dome of the old capitol showed above the water-maple trees, and Dugmore clanking straight ahead, with a string of negroes and boys and the sheriff following along behind him. Under the shadow of a quarried-out hillside a gate opened in a high stone wall to admit him into life membership with a white-and-black-striped brotherhood of shame.

Four years there did the work for the gangling, silent mountaineer. One day, just before the Christmas holidays, the new governor of the state paid a visit to the prison. Only his private secretary came with him. The warden showed them through the cell houses, the workshops, the dining hall and the walled yards. It was a Sunday afternoon; the white prisoners loafed in their stockade, the blacks in theirs. In a corner on the white side, where the thin and skimpy winter sunshine slanted over the stockade wall, Anse Dugmore was squatted; merely a rack of bones enclosed in a shapeless covering of black-and-white stripes. On his close-cropped head and over his cheekbones the skin was stretched so tight it seemed nearly ready to split. His eyes, glassy and bleared with pain, stared ahead of him with a sick man's fixed stare. Inside his convict's cotton shirt his chest was caved away almost to nothing, and from the collarless neckband his neck rose as bony as a plucked fowl's, with great, blue cords in it. Lacking a coverlet to pick, his fingers picked at the skin on his retreating chin.

As the governor stood in an arched doorway watching, the lengthening afternoon shadow edged along and covered the hunkered-down figure by the wall. Anse tottered to his feet, moved a few inches so that he might still be in the sunshine, and settled down again. This small exertion started a cough that threatened to tear him apart. He drew his hand across his mouth and a red stain came away on the knotty knuckles. The warden was a kindly enough man in the ordinary relations of life, but nine years as a tamer of man-beasts in a great stone cage had overlaid his sympathies with a thickening callus.

"One of our lifers that we won't have with us much longer," he said casually, noting that the governor's eyes followed the sick convict. "When the con gets one of these hill billies he goes mighty fast."

"A mountaineer, then?" said the governor. "What's his name?"

"Dugmore," answered the warden; "sent from Clayton County. One of those Clayton County feud fighters."

The governor nodded understandingly. "What sort of a record has he made here?"

"Oh, fair enough!" said the warden. "Those man-killers from the mountains generally make good prisoners. Funny thing about this fellow, though. All the time he's been here he never, so far as I know, had a message or a visitor or a line of writing from the outside. Nor wrote a letter out himself. Nor made friends with anybody, convict or guard."

"Has he applied for a pardon?" asked the governor.

"Lord, no!" said the warden. "When he was well he just took what was coming to him, the same as he's taking it now. I can look up his record, though, if you'd care to see it, sir."

"I believe I should," said the governor quietly.

A spectacled young wife-murderer, who worked in the prison office on the prison books, got down a book and looked through it until he came to a certain entry on a certain page. The warden was right — so far as the black marks of the prison discipline went, the friendless convict's record showed fair.

"I think," said the young governor to the warden and his secretary when they had moved out of hearing of the convict bookkeeper — "I think I'll give that poor devil a pardon for a Christmas gift. It's no more than a mercy to let him die at home, if he has any home to go to."

"I could have him brought in and let you tell him yourself, sir," volunteered the warden.

"No, no," said the governor quickly. "I don't want to hear that cough again. Nor look on such a wreck," he added.

Two days before Christmas the warden sent to the hospital ward for No. 874. No. 874, that being Anse Dugmore, came shuffling in and kept himself upright by holding with one hand to the door jamb. The warden sat rotund and impressive, in a swivel chair, holding in his hands a folded-up, blue-backed document.

"Dugmore," he said in his best official manner, "when His Excellency, Governor Woodford, was here on Sunday he took notice that your general health was not good. So, of his own accord, he has sent you an unconditional pardon for a Christmas gift, and here it is."

The sick convict's eyes, between their festering lids, fixed on the warden's face and a sudden light flickered in their pale, glazed shallows; but he didn't speak. There was a little pause.

"I said the governor has given you a pardon," repeated the warden, staring hard at him.

"I heered you the fust time," croaked the prisoner in his eaten-out voice. "When kin I go?"

"Is that all you've got to say?" demanded the warden, bristling up.

"I said, when kin I go?" repeated No. 874.

"Go! — you can go now. You can't go too soon to suit me!"

The warden swung his chair around and showed him the broad of his indignant back. When he had filled out certain forms at his desk he shoved a pen into the silent consumptive's fingers and showed him crossly where to make his mark. At a signal from his bent forefinger a negro trusty came forward and took the pardoned man away and helped him put his shrunken limbs into a suit of the prison-made slops, of cheap, black shoddy, with the taint of a jail thick and heavy on it. A deputy warden thrust into Dugmore's hands a railroad ticket and the five dollars that the law requires shall be given to a freed felon. He took them without a word and, still without a word, stepped out of the gate that swung open for him and into a light, spitty snowstorm. With the inbred instinct of the hillsman he swung about and headed for the little, light-blue station at the head of the crooked street. He went slowly, coughing often as the cold air struck into his wasted lungs, and sometimes staggering up against the fences. Through a barred window the wondering warden sourly watched the crawling, tottery figure.

"Damned savage!" he said to himself. "Didn't even say thank you. I'll bet he never had any more feelings or sentiments in his life than a moccasin snake."

Something to the same general effect was expressed a few minutes later by a brakeman who had just helped a wofully feeble passenger aboard the eastbound train and had steered him, staggering and gasping from weakness, to a seat at the forward end of an odorous red-plush day coach.

"Just a bundle of bones held together by a skin," the brakeman was saying to the conductor, "and the smell of the pen all over him. Never said a word to me — just looked at me sort of dumb. Bound for plumb up at the far end of the division, accordin' to the way his ticket reads. I doubt if he lives to get there."

The warden and the brakeman both were wrong. The freed man did live to get there. And it was an emotion which the warden had never suspected that held life in him all that afternoon and through the comfortless night in the packed and noisome day coach, while the fussy, self-sufficient little train went looping, like an overgrown measuring worm, up through the blue grass, around the outlying knobs of the foothills, on and on through the great riven chasm of the gateway into a bleak, bare clutch of undersized mountains. Anse Dugmore had two bad hemorrhages on the way, but he lived.

Under the full moon of a white and flawless night before Christmas, Shem Dugmore's squatty log cabin made a blot on the thin blanket of snow, and inside the one room of the cabin Shem Dugmore sat alone by the daubed-clay hearth, glooming. Hours passed and he hardly moved except to stir the red coals or kick back some ambitious ember of hickory that leaped out upon the uneven floor. Suddenly something heavy fell limply against the locked door, and instantly, all alertness, the shock-headed mountaineer was backed up against the farther wall, out of range of the two windows, with his weapons drawn, silent, ready for what might come. After a minute there was a feeble, faint pecking sound — half knock, half scratch — at the lower part of the door. It might have been a wornout dog or any spent wild creature, but no line of Shem Dugmore's figure relaxed, and under his thick, sandy brows his eyes, in the flickering light, had the greenish shine of an angry cat-animal's.

"Whut is it?" he called. "And whut do you want? Speak out peartly!"

The answer came through the thick planking thinly, in a sort of gasping whine that ended in a chattering cough; but even after Shem's ear caught the words, and even after he recognized the changed but still familiar cadence of the voice, he abated none of his caution. Carefully he unbolted the door, and, drawing it inch by inch slowly ajar, he reached out, exposing only his hand and arm, and drew bodily inside the shell of a man that was fallen, huddled up, against the log door jamb. He dropped the wooden crossbar back into its sockets before he looked a second time at the intruder, who had crawled across the floor and now lay before the wide mouth of the hearth in a choking spell. Shem Dugmore made no move until the fit was over and the sufferer lay quiet.

"How did you git out, Anse?" were the first words he spoke.

The consumptive rolled his head weakly from side to side and swallowed desperately. "Pardoned out — in writin' — yistiddy."

"You air in purty bad shape," said Shem.

"Yes," — the words came very slowly — "my lungs give out on me — and my eyes. But — but I got here."

"You come jist in time," said his cousin; "this time tomorrer and you wouldn't a' never found me here. I'd 'a' been gone."

"Gone! — gone whar?"

"Well," said Shem slowly, "after you was sent away it seemed like them Tranthams got the upper hand complete. All of our side whut ain't dead — and that's powerful few — is moved off out of the mountings to Winchester, down in the settlemints. I'm 'bout the last, and I'm a-purposin' to slip out tomorrer night while the Tranthams is at their Christmas rackets — they'd layway me too ef —"

"But my wife — did she —"

"I thought maybe you'd heered tell about that whilst you was down yon," said Shem in a dulled wonder. "The fall after you was took away yore woman she went over to the Tranthams. Yes, sir; she took up with the head devil of 'em all — old Wyatt Trantham hisself — and she went to live at his house up on the Yaller Banks."

"Is she — Did she —"

The ex-convict was struggling to his knees. His groping skeletons of hands were right in the hot ashes. The heat cooked the moisture from his sodden garments in little films of vapor and filled the cabin with the reek of the prison dye.

"Did she — did she —"

"Oh, she's been dead quite a spell now," stated Shem. "I would have s'posed you'd 'a' heered that, too, somewhars. She had a kind of a risin' in the breast."

"But my young uns — little Anderson and — and Elviry?"

The sick man was clear up on his knees now, his long arms hanging and his eyes, behind their matted lids, fixed on Shem's impassive face. Could the warden have seen him now, and marked his attitude and his words, he would have known what it was that had brought this dying man back to *his* own mountain valley with the breath of life still in him. A dumb, unuttered love for the two shock-headed babies he had left behind in the split-board cabin was the one big thing in Anse Dugmore's whole being — bigger even than his sense of allegiance to the feud.

"My young uns, Shem?"

"Wyatt Trantham took 'em and he kep' 'em — he's got 'em both now."

"Does he — does he use 'em kindly?"

"I ain't never heered," said Shem simply. "He never had no young uns of his own, and it mout be he uses 'em well. He's the high sheriff now."

"I was countin' on gittin' to see 'em agin — an buyin 'em some little Chrismus fixin's," the father wheezed. Hopelessness was coming into his rasping whisper. "I reckon it ain't no use to — to be thinkin' — of that there now?"

"No 'arthly use at all," said Shem, with brutal directness. "Ef you had the strength to git thar, the Tranthams would shoot you down like a fice dog."

Anse nodded weakly. He sank down again on the floor, face to the boards, coughing hard. It was the droning voice of his cousin that brought him back from the borders of the coma he had been fighting off for hours.

For, to Shem, the best hater and the poorest fighter of all his cleaned-out clan, had come a great thought. He shook the drowsing man and roused him, and plied him with sips from a dipper of the unhallowed white corn whisky of a mountain still-house. And as he worked over him he told off the tally of the last four years: of the uneven, unmerciful war, ticking off on his blunt finger ends the grim totals of this one ambushed and that one killed in the open, overpowered and beaten under by weight of odds. He told such details as he knew of the theft of the young wife and the young ones, Elvira and little Anderson.

"Anse, did ary Trantham see you a-gittin' here tonight?"

"Nobody — that knowed me — seed me."

"Old Wyatt Trantham, he rid into Manchester this evenin' 'bout fo' o'clock — I seed him passin' over the ridge," went on Shem. "He'll be ridin' back 'long Pigeon Roost some time before mawnin'. He done you a heap o' dirt, Anse."

The prostrate man was listening hard.

"Anse, I got yore old rifle right here in the house. Ef you could git up thar on the mounting, somewhar's alongside the Pigeon Roost trail, you could git him shore. He'll be full of licker comin' back."

And now a seeming marvel was coming to pass, for the caved-in trunk was rising on the pipestem legs and the shaking fingers were outstretched, reaching for something.

Shem stepped lightly to a corner of the cabin and brought forth a rifle and began reloading it afresh from a box of shells.

A wavering figure crept across the small stump-dotted "dead'ning" — Anse Dugmore was upon his errand. He dragged the rifle by the barrel, so that its butt made a crooked, broken furrow in the new snow like the trail of a crippled snake. He fell and got up, and fell and rose again. He coughed and up the ridge a ranging dog-fox barked back an answer to his cough.

From out of the slitted door Shem watched him until the scrub oaks at the edge of the clearing swallowed him up. Then Shem fastened himself in and made ready to start his flight to the lowlands that very night.

Just below the forks of Pigeon Roost Creek the trail that followed its banks widened into a track wide enough for wagon wheels. On one side lay the diminished creek, now filmed over with a glaze of young ice. On the other the mountain rose steeply. Fifteen feet up the bluff side a fallen dead tree projected its rotted, broken roots, like snaggled teeth, from the clayey bank. Behind this tree's trunk, in the snow and half-frozen, half-melted yellow mire, Anse Dugmore was stretched on his face. The barrel of the rifle barely showed itself through the interlacing root ends. It pointed downward and northward toward the broad, moonlit place in the road. Its stock was pressed tightly against Anse Dugmore's fallen-in cheek; the trigger finger of his right hand, fleshless as a joint of cane, was crooked about the trigger guard. A thin stream of blood ran from his mouth and dribbled down his chin and coagulated in a sticky smear upon the gun stock. His lungs, what was left of them, were draining away.

He lay without motion, saving up the last ounce of his life. The cold had crawled up his legs to his hips; he was dead already from the waist down. He no longer coughed, only gasped thickly. He knew that he was about gone; but he knew, too, that he would last, clear-minded and clear-eyed, until High Sheriff Wyatt Trantham came. His brain would last — and his trigger finger.

Then he heard him coming. Up the trail sounded the muffled music of a pacer's hoofs single-footing through the snow, and after that, almost instantly Trantham rode out into sight and loomed larger and larger as he drew steadily near the open place under the bank. He was wavering in the saddle. He drew nearer and nearer, and as he came out on the wide patch of moonlit snow, he pulled the single-footer down to a walk and halted him and began fumbling in the right-hand side of the saddlebags that draped his horse's shoulder.

Up in its covert the rifle barrel moved an inch or two, then steadied and stopped, the bone-sight at its tip resting full on the broad of the drunken rider's breast. The boney finger moved inward from the trigger guard and closed ever so gently about the touchy, hair-filed trigger — then waited.

For the uncertain hand of Trantham, every movement showing plain in the crystal, hard, white moon, was slowly bringing from under the flap of the right-side saddlebag something that was round and smooth and shone with a yellowish glassy light, like a fat flask filled with spirits. And Anse Dugmore waited, being minded now to shoot him as he put the bottle to his lips, and so cheat Trantham of his last drink on earth, as Trantham had cheated him of his liberty and his babies — as Trantham had cheated those babies of the Christmas fixings which the state's five dollars might have bought.

He waited, waited —

———

This was not the first time the high sheriff had stopped that night on his homeward ride from the tiny county seat, as his befuddlement proclaimed; but halting there in the open, just past the forks of the Pigeon Roost, he was moved by a new idea. He fumbled in the right-hand flap of his saddlebags and brought out a toy drum, round and smooth, with shiny yellow sides. A cheap china doll with painted black ringlets and painted blue eyes followed the drum, and then a torn paper bag, from which small pieces of cheap red-and-green dyed candy sifted out between the sheriff's fumbling fingers and fell into the snow.

Thirty feet away, in the dead leaves matted under the roots of an uptorn dead tree, something moved — something moved; and then there was a sound like a long, deep, gurgling sigh, and another sound like some heavy, lengthy object settling itself down flat upon the snow and the leaves.

The first faint rustle cleared Trantham's brain of the liquor fumes. He jammed the toys and the candy back into the saddlebags and jerked his horse sidewise into the protecting shadow of the bluff, reaching at the same time to the shoulder holster buckled about his body under the unbuttoned overcoat. For a long minute he listened keenly, the drawn pistol in his hand. There was nothing to hear except his own breathing and the breathing of his horse.

"Sho! Some old hawg turnin' over in her bed," he said to the horse, and holstering the pistol he went racking on down Pigeon Roost Creek, with Christmas for Elviry and little Anderson in his saddlebags.

When they found Anse Dugmore in his ambush another snow had fallen on his back and he was slightly more of a skeleton than ever; but the bony finger was still crooked about the trigger, the rusted hammer was back at full cock and there was a dried brownish stain on the gun stock. So, from these facts, his finders were moved to conclude that the freed convict must have bled to death from his lungs before the sheriff ever passed, which they held to be a good thing all round and a lucky thing for the sheriff.

VII

TO THE EDITOR
OF THE SUN

There was a sound, heard in the early hours of a
Sunday morning, that used to bother strangers in our town
until they got used to it. It started usually along about half
past five or six o'clock and it kept up interminably — so it
seemed to them — a monotonous, jarring thump-thump,
thump-thump that was like the far-off beating of African
tomtoms; but at breakfast, when the beaten biscuits came
upon the table, throwing off a steamy hot halo of their own
goodness, these aliens knew what it was that had roused
them, and, unless they were dyspeptics by nature, felt
amply recompensed for the lost hours of their beauty sleep.

In these degenerate latter days I believe there is a
machine that accomplishes the same purpose noiselessly by
a process of rolling and crushing, which no doubt is
efficacious; but it seems somehow to take the poetry out of
the operation. Old Judge Priest, our circuit judge, and the
reigning black deity of his kitchen, Aunt Dilsey Turner,
would have naught of it. So long as his digestion survived
and her good right arm held out to endure, there would be
real beaten biscuits for the judge's Sunday morning
breakfast. And so, having risen with the dawn or a little
later, Aunt Dilsey, wielding a maul-headed tool of whittled
wood, would pound the dough with rhythmic strokes until
it was as plastic as sculptor's modeling clay and as light as
eiderdown, full of tiny hills and hollows, in which small
yeasty bubbles rose and spread and burst like foam
globules on the flanks of gentle wavelets. Then, with her
master hand, she would roll it thin and cut out the small
round disks and delicately pink each one with a fork — and

then, if you were listening, you could hear the stove door slam like the smacking of an iron lip.

On a certain Sunday I have in mind, Judge Priest woke with the first premonitory thud from the kitchen, and he was up and dressed in his white linens and out upon the wide front porch while the summer day was young and unblemished. The sun was not up good yet. It made a red glow, like a barn afire, through the treetops looking eastward. Lie-abed blackbirds were still talking over family matters in the maples that clustered round the house, and in the back yard Judge Priest's big red rooster hoarsely circulated gossip in regard to a certain little brown hen, first crowing out the news loudly and then listening, with his head on one side, while the rooster in the next yard took it up and repeated it to a rooster living farther down the road, as is the custom among male scandalizers the world over. Upon the lawn the little gossamer hammocks that the grass spiders had seamed together overnight were spangled with dew, so that each out-thrown thread was a glittering rosary and the center of each web a silken, cushioned jewel casket. Likewise each web was outlined in white mist, for the cottonwood trees were shedding down their podded product so thickly that across open spaces the slanting lines of the drifting fiber looked like snow. It would be hot enough after a while, but now the whole world was sweet and fresh and washed clean.

It impressed Judge Priest so. He lowered his bulk into a rustic chair made of hickory withes that gave to his weight, and put his thoughts upon breakfast and the goodness of the day; but presently, as he sat there, he saw something that set a frown between his faded blue eyes.

He saw, coming down Clay Street, upon the opposite side, an old man — a very feeble old man — who was tall and thin and dressed in somber black. The man was lame — he dragged one leg along with the hitching gait of the paralytic. Traveling with painful slowness, he came on until he reached the corner above. Then automatically he turned at right angles and left the narrow wooden sidewalk and crossed the dusty road. He passed Judge Priest's, looking neither to the right nor the left, and so kept on until he reached the corner below. Still following an invisible path in the deep-furrowed dust, he crossed again to the other side. Just as he got there his halt leg seemed to give out altogether and for a minute or two he stood holding himself up by a fumbling grip upon the slats of a tree box before he went laboriously on, a figure of pain and weakness in the early sunshine that was now beginning to slant across his path and dapple his back with checkerings of shadow and light.

This maneuver was inexplicable — a stranger would have puzzled to make it out. The shade was as plentiful upon one side of Clay Street as upon the other; each sagged wooden sidewalk was in as bad repair as its brother over the way. The small, shabby frame house, buried in honeysuckles and balsam vines, which stood close up to the pavement line on the opposite side of Clay Street, facing Judge Priest's roomy and rambling old home, had no flag of pestilence at its door or its window. And surely to this lone pedestrian every added step must have been an added labor. A stranger would never have understood it; but Judge Priest understood it — he had seen that same thing repeated countless times in the years that stretched behind him. Always it had distressed him inwardly, but on this particular morning it distressed him more than ever. The toiling grim figure in black had seemed so feeble and so tottery and old.

Well, Judge Priest was not exactly what you would call young. With an effort he heaved himself up out of the depths of his hickory chair and stood at the edge of his porch, polishing a pink bald dome of forehead as though trying to make up his mind to something. Jefferson

Poindexter, resplendent in starchy white jacket and white apron, came to the door.

"Breakfus' served, suh!" he said, giving to an announcement touching on food that glamour of grandeur of which his race alone enjoys the splendid secret.

"Hey?" asked the judge absently.

"Breakfus' — hit's on the table waitin', suh," stated Jeff. "Mizz Polks sent over her houseboy with a dish of fresh razberries fur yore breakfus'; and she say to tell you, with her and Mistah Polkses' compliments, they is fresh picked out of her garden — specially fur you."

The lady and gentleman to whom Jeff had reference were named Polk, but in speaking of white persons for whom he had a high regard Jeff always, wherever possible within the limitations of our speech, tacked on that final s. It was in the nature of a delicate verbal compliment, implying that the person referred to was worthy of enlargement and pluralization.

Alone in the cool, high-ceiled, white-walled dining room, Judge Priest ate his breakfast mechanically. The raspberries were pink beads of sweetness; the young fried chicken was a poem in delicate and flaky browns; the spoon bread could not have been any better if it had tried; and the beaten biscuits were as light as snowflakes and as ready to melt on the tongue; but Judge Priest spoke hardly a word all through the meal. Jeff, going out to the kitchen for the last course, said to Aunt Dilsey:

"Ole boss-man seem lak he's got somethin' on his mind worryin' him this mawnin'."

When Jeff returned, with a turn of crisp waffles in one hand and a pitcher of cane sirup in the other, he stared in surprise, for the dining room was empty and he could hear his employer creaking down the hall. Jeff just naturally hated to see good hot waffles going to waste. He ate them himself, standing up; and they gave him a zest for his regular breakfast, which followed in due course of time.

From the old walnut hatrack, with its white-tipped knobs that stood just inside the front door, Judge Priest picked up a palmleaf fan; and he held the fan slantwise as a shield for his eyes and his bare head against the sun's glare as he went down the porch steps and passed out of his own yard, traversed the empty street and strove with the stubborn gate latch of the little house that faced his own. It was a poor-looking little house, and its poorness had extended to its surroundings — as if poverty was a contagion that spread. In Judge Priest's yard, now, the grass, though uncared for, yet grew thick and lush; but here, in this small yard, there were bare, shiny spots of earth showing through the grass — as though the soil itself was out at elbows and the nap worn off its green-velvet coat; but the vines about the porch were thick enough for an ambuscade and from behind their green screen came a voice in hospitable recognition.

"Is that you, judge? Well sir, I'm glad to see you! Come right in; take a seat and sit down and rest yourself."

The speaker showed himself in the arched opening of the vine barrier — an old man — not quite so old, perhaps, as the judge. He was in his shirtsleeves. There was a patch upon one of the sleeves. His shoes had been newly shined, but the job was poorly done; the leather showed a dulled black upon the toes and a weathered yellow at the sides and heels. As he spoke his voice ran up and down — the voice of a deaf person who cannot hear his own words clearly, so that he pitches them in a false key. For added proof of this affliction he held a lean and slightly tremulous hand cupped behind his ear.

The other hand he extended in greeting as the old judge mounted the step of the low porch. The visitor took one of two creaky wooden rockers that stood in the narrow space behind the balsam vines, and for a minute or two he sat without speech, fanning himself. Evidently these neighborly calls between these two old men were not uncommon; they could enjoy the communion of silence together without embarrassment.

The town clocks struck — first the one on the city hall struck eight times sedately; and then, farther away, the one on the county courthouse. This one struck five times slowly, hesitated a moment, struck eleven times with great vigor, hesitated again, struck once with a big, final boom, and was through. No amount of repairing could cure the courthouse clock of this peculiarity. It kept the time, but kept it according to a private way of its own. Immediately after it ceased the bell on the Catholic church, first and earliest of the Sunday bells, began tolling briskly. Judge Priest waited until its clamoring had died away.

"Goin' to be good and hot after while," he said, raising his voice.

"What say?"

"I say it's goin' to be mighty warm a little later on in the day," repeated Judge Priest.

"Yes, suh; I reckon you're right there," assented the host. "Just a minute ago, before you came over, I was telling Liddie she'd find it middlin' close in church this morning. She's going, though — runaway horses wouldn't keep her away from church! I'm not going myself — seems as though I'm getting more and more out of the church habit here lately."

Judge Priest's eyes squinted in whimsical appreciation of this admission. He remembered that the other man, during the lifetime of his second wife, had been a regular attendant at services — going twice on Sundays and to Wednesday night prayer meetings too; but the second wife had been dead going on four years now — or was it five? Time sped so!

The deaf man spoke on:

"So I just thought I'd sit here and try to keep cool and wait for that Ledbetter boy to come round with the Sunday paper. Did you read last Sunday's paper, judge? Colonel

Watterson certainly had a mighty fine piece on those Northern money devils. It's round here somewhere — I cut it out to keep it. I'd like to have you read it and pass your opinion on it. These young fellows do pretty well, but there's none of them can write like the colonel, in my judgment."

Judge Priest appeared not to have heard him.

"Ed Tilghman," he said abruptly in his high, fine voice, that seemed absurdly out of place, coming from his round frame, "you and me have lived neighbors together a good while, haven't we? We've been right acros't the street from one another all this time. It kind of jolts me sometimes when I git to thinkin' how many years it's really been; because we're gittin' along right smartly in years — all us old fellows are. Ten years from now, say, there won't be so many of us left." He glanced sidewise at the lean, firm profile of his friend. "You're younger than some of us; but, even so, you ain't exactly what I'd call a young man yourself."

Avoiding the direct, questioning gaze that his companion turned on him at this, the judge reached forward and touched a ripe balsam apple that dangled in front of him. Instantly it split, showing the gummed red seeds clinging to the inner walls of the sensitive pod.

"I'm listening to you, judge," said the deaf man.

For a moment the old judge waited. There was about him almost an air of embarrassment. Still considering the ruin of the balsam apple, he spoke, and it was with a sort of hurried anxiety, as though he feared he might be checked before he could say what he had to say.

"Ed," he said, "I was settin' on my porch a while ago waitin' for breakfast, and your brother came by." He shot a quick, apprehensive glance at his silent auditor. Except for a tautened flickering of the muscles about the mouth, there was no sign that the other had heard him. "Your brother Abner came by," repeated the judge, "and I set over there on my porch and watched him pass. Ed, Abner's gittin' mighty feeble! He jest about kin drag himself along — he's had another stroke lately, they tell me. He had to hold on to that there treebox down yonder, steadyin' himself after he crossed back over to this side. Lord knows what he was doin' draggin' down-town on a Sunday mornin' — force of habit, I reckin. Anyway he certainly did look older and more poorly than ever I saw him before. He's a failin' man if I'm any judge. Do you hear me plain?" he asked.

"I hear you," said his neighbor in a curiously flat voice. It was Tilghman's turn to avoid the glances of his friend. He stared straight ahead of him through a rift in the vines.

"Well, then," went on Judge Priest, "here's what I've got to say to you, Ed Tilghman. You know as well as I do that I've never pried into your private affairs, and it goes mightily against the grain for me to be doin' so now; but, Ed, when I think of how old we're all gittin' to be, and when the Camp meets and I see you settin' there side by side almost, and yet never seemin' to see each other — and this mornin' when I saw Abner pass, lookin' so gaunt and sick — and it sech a sweet, ca'm mornin' too, and everything so quiet and peaceful —" He broke off and started anew. "I don't seem to know exactly how to put my thoughts into words — and puttin' things into words is supposed to be my trade too. Anyway I couldn't go to Abner. He's not my neighbor and you are; and besides, you're the youngest of the two. So — so I came over here to you. Ed, I'd like mightily to take some word from you to your brother Abner. I'd like to do it the best in the world! Can't I go to him with a message from you — today? Tomorrow might be too late!"

He laid one of his pudgy hands on the bony knee of the deaf man; but the hand slipped away as Tilghman stood up.

"Judge Priest," said Tilghman, looking down at him, "I've listened to what you've had to say; and I didn't stop you, because you are my friend and I know you mean well by it. Besides, you're my guest, under my own roof." He stumped back and forth in the narrow confines of the porch. Otherwise he gave no sign of any emotion that might be astir within him, his face being still set and his voice flat. "What's between me and my — what's between me and that man you just named always will be between us. He's satisfied to let things go on as they are. I'm satisfied to let them go on. It's in our breed, I guess. Words — just words — wouldn't help mend this thing. The reason for it would be there just the same, and neither one of us is going to be able to forget that so long as we both live. I'd just as soon you never brought this — this subject up again. If you went to him I presume he'd tell you the same thing. Let it be, Judge Priest — it's past mending. We two have gone on this way for fifty years nearly. We'll keep on going on so. I appreciate your kindness, Judge Priest; but let it be — let it be!"

There was finality miles deep and fixed as basalt in his tone. He checked his walk and called in at a shuttered window.

"Liddie," he said in his natural up-and-down voice, "before you put off for church, couldn't you mix up a couple of lemonades or something? Judge Priest is out here on the porch with me."

"No," said Judge Priest, getting slowly up, "I've got to be gittin' back before the sun's up too high. If I don't see you again meanwhile be shore to come to the next regular meetin' of the Camp — on Friday night," he added.

"I'll be there," said Tilghman. "And I'll try to find that piece of Colonel Watterson's and send it over to you. I'd like mightily for you to read it."

He stood at the opening in the vines, with one slightly palsied hand fumbling at a loose tendril as the judge passed down the short yard-walk and out at the gate. Then he went back to his chair and sat down again. All those little muscles in his jowls were jumping.

Clay Street was no longer empty. Looking down its dusty length from beneath the shelter of his palmleaf fan, Judge Priest saw here and there groups of children — the little girls in prim and starchy white, the little boys hobbling in the Sunday torment of shoes and stockings; and all of them were moving toward a common center — Sunday school. Twice again that day would the street show life — a little later when grown-ups went their way to church, and again just after the noonday dinner, when young people and servants, carrying trays and dishes under napkins, would cross and recross from one house to another. The Sunday interchange of special dainties between neighbors amounted in our town to a ceremonial and a rite; but after that, until the cool of the evening, the town would simmer in quiet, while everybody took Sunday naps.

With his fan, Judge Priest made an angry sawing motion in the air, as though trying to fend off something disagreeable — a memory, perhaps, or it might have been only a persistent midge. There were plenty of gnats and midges about, for by now — even so soon — the dew was dried. The leaves of the silver poplars were turning their white under sides up like countless frog bellies, and the long, podded pendants of the Injun-cigar trees hung dangling and still. It would be a hot day, sure enough; already the judge felt wilted and worn out.

In our town we had our tragedies that endured for years and, in the small-town way, finally became institutions. There was the case of the Burnleys. For thirty-odd years old Major Burnley lived on one side of his house and his wife lived on the other, neither of them ever crossing an imaginary dividing line that ran down the middle of the hall, having for their medium of intercourse all that time a lean, spinster daughter, in whose gray and barren life churchwork and these strange home duties took the place that Nature had intended to be filled by a husband and by babies and grandbabies.

There was crazy Saul Vance, in his garb of a fantastic scarecrow, who was forever starting somewhere and never going there — because, as sure as he came to a place where two roads crossed, he could not make up his mind which turn to take. In his youth a girl had jilted him, or a bank had failed on him, or a horse had kicked him in the head — or maybe it was all three of these things that had addled his poor brains. Anyhow he went his pitiable, aimless way for years, taunted daily by small boys who were more cruel than jungle beasts. How he lived nobody knew, but when he died some of the men who as boys had jeered him turned out to be his volunteer pallbearers.

There was Mr. H. Jackman — Brother Jackman to all the town — who had been our leading hatter once and rich besides, and in the days of his affluence had given the Baptist church its bells. In his old age, when he was dog-poor, he lived on charity, only it was not known by that word, which is at once the sweetest and bitterest word in our tongue; for Brother Jackman, always primped, always plump and well clad, would go through the market to take his pick of what was there, and to the Richland House bar for his toddies, and to Felsburg Brothers for new garments when his old ones wore shabby — and yet never paid a cent for anything; a kindly conspiracy on the part of the whole town enabling him to maintain his self-respect to the last. Strangers in our town used to take him for a retired banker — that's a fact!

And there was old man Stackpole, who had killed his man — had killed him in fair fight and had been acquitted — and yet walked quiet back streets at all hours, a gray, silent shadow, and never slept except with a bright light burning in his room.

The tragedy of Mr. Edward Tilghman, though, and of Captain Abner G. Tilghman, his elder brother, was both a tragedy and a mystery — the biggest tragedy and the deepest mystery our town had ever known or ever would know probably. All that anybody knew for certain was that for upward of fifty years neither of them had spoken to the other, nor by deed or look had given heed to the other. As boys, back in sixty-one, they had gone out together. Side by side, each with his arm over the other's shoulder, they had stood up with a hundred others to be sworn into the service of the Confederate States of America; and on the morning they went away Miss Sally May Ghoulson had given the older brother her silk scarf off her shoulders to wear for a sash. Both the brothers had liked her; but by this public act she made it plain which of them was her choice.

Then the company had marched off to the camp on the Tennessee border, where the new troops were drilling; and as they marched some watchers wept and others cheered — but the cheering predominated, for it was to be only a sort of picnic anyhow — so everybody agreed. As the orators — who mainly stayed behind — had pointed out, the Northern people would not fight. And even if they should fight could not one Southerner whip four Yankees? Certainly he could; any fool knew that much. In a month or two months, or at most three months, they would all be tramping home again, covered with glory and the spoils of war, and then — this by common report and understanding — Miss Sally May Ghoulson and Abner Tilghman would be married, with a big church wedding.

The Yankees, however, unaccountably fought, and it was not a ninety-day picnic after all. It was not any kind of a picnic. And when it was over, after four years and a month, Miss Sally May Ghoulson and Abner Tilghman did not marry. It was just before the battle of Chickamauga when the other men in the company first noticed that the two Tilghmans had become as strangers, and worse than strangers, to each other. They quit speaking to each other then and there, and to any man's knowledge they never spoke again. They served the war out, Abner rising just before the end to a captaincy, Edward serving always as a private in the ranks. In a dour, grim silence they took the fortunes of those last hard, hopeless days and after the surrender down in Mississippi they came back with the limping handful that was left of the company; and in age they were all boys still — but in experience, men, and in suffering, grandsires.

Two months after they got back Miss Sally May Ghoulson was married to Edward, the younger brother. Within a year she died, and after a decent period of mourning Edward married a second time — only to be widowed again after many years. His second wife bore him children and they died — all except one, a daughter, who grew up and married badly; and after her mother's death she came back to live with her deaf father and minister to him. As for Captain Abner Tilghman, he never married — never, so far as the watching eyes of the town might tell, looked with favor upon another woman. And he never spoke to his brother or to any of his brother's family — or his brother to him.

With years the wall of silence they had builded up between them turned to ice and the ice to stone. They lived on the same street, but never did Edward enter Captain Abner's bank, never did Captain Abner pass Edward's house — always he crossed over to the opposite side. They belonged to the same Veterans' Camp — indeed there was only the one for them to belong to; they voted the same ticket — straight Democratic; and in the same church, the old Independent Presbyterian, they worshiped the same God by the same creed, the older brother being an elder and the younger a plain member — and yet never crossed looks.

The town had come to accept this dumb and bitter feud as unchangeable and eternal; in time people ceased even to wonder what its cause had been, and in all the long years only one man had tried, before now, to heal it up. When old Doctor Henrickson died, a young and ardent clergyman, fresh from the Virginia theological school, came out to take the vacant pulpit; and he, being filled with a high sense of his holy calling, thought it shameful that such a thing should be in the congregation. He went to see Captain Tilghman about it. He never went but that once. Afterward it came out that Captain Tilghman had threatened to walk out of church and never darken its doors again if the minister ever dared to mention his brother's name in his presence. So the young minister sorrowed, but obeyed, for the captain was rich and a generous giver to the church.

And he had grown richer with the years, and as he grew richer his brother grew poorer — another man owned the drug store where Edward Tilghman had failed. They had grown from young to middle-aged men and from middle-aged men to old, infirm men; and first the grace of youth and then the solidness of maturity had gone out of them and the gnarliness of age had come upon them; one was halt of step and the other was dull of ear; and the town through half a century of schooling had accustomed itself to the situation and took it as a matter of course. So it was and so it always would be — a tragedy and a mystery. It had not been of any use when the minister interfered and it was of no use now. Judge Priest, with the gesture of a man who is beaten, dropped the fan on the porch floor, went into his darkened sitting room, stretched himself wearily on a creaking horsehide sofa and called out to Jeff to make him a mild toddy — one with plenty of ice in it.

On this same Sunday — or, anyhow, I like to fancy it was on this same Sunday — at a point distant approximately nine hundred and seventy miles in a northeasterly direction from Judge Priest's town, Corporal Jacob Speck, late of Sigel's command, sat at the kitchen window of the combined Speck and Engel apartment on

East Eighty-fifth Street in the Borough of Manhattan, New York. He was in his shirtsleeves; his tender feet were incased in a pair of red-and-green carpet slippers. In the angle of his left arm he held his youngest grandchild, aged one and a half years, while his right hand carefully poised a china pipe, with a bowl like an egg-cup and a stem like a fishpole. The corporal's blue Hanoverian eyes, behind their thick-lensed glasses, were fixed upon a comprehensive vista of East Eighty-fifth Street back yards and clothespoles and fire escapes; but his thoughts were very much elsewhere.

Reared back there at seeming ease, the corporal none the less was not happy in his mind. It was not that he so much minded being left at home to mind the youngest baby while the rest of the family spent the afternoon amid the Teutonic splendors of Smeltzer's Harlem River Casino, with its acres of gravel walks and its whitewashed tree trunks, its straggly flower beds and its high-collared beers. He was used to that sort of thing. Since a plague of multiplying infirmities of the body had driven him out of his job in the tax office, the corporal had not done much except nurse the babies that occurred in the Speck-Engel establishment with such unerring regularity. Sometimes, it is true, he did slip down to the corner for maybe zwei glasses of beer and a game of pinocle; but then, likely as not, there would come inopportunely a towheaded descendant to tell him Mommer needed him back at the flat right away to mind the baby while she went marketing or to the movies.

He could endure that — he had to. What riled Corporal Jacob Speck on this warm and sunny Sunday was a realization that he was not doing his share at making the history of the period. The week before had befallen the fiftieth anniversary of the marching away of his old regiment to the front; there had been articles in the daily papers about it. Also, in patriotic commemoration of the great event there had been a parade of the wrinkled survivors — ninety-odd of them — following their tattered and faded battle flag down Fifth Avenue past apathetic crowds, nine-tenths of whom had been born since the war — in foreign lands mainly; and at least half, if one might judge by their looks, did not know what the parading was all about, and did not particularly care either.

The corporal had not participated in the march of the veterans; he had not even attended the banquet that followed it. True, the youngest grandchild was at the moment cutting one of her largest jaw teeth and so had required, for the time, an extraordinary and special amount of minding; but the young lady's dental difficulty was not the sole reason for his absence. Three weeks earlier the corporal had taken part in Decoration Day, and certainly one parade a month was ample strain upon a pair of legs such as he owned. He had returned home with his game leg behaving more gamely then usual and with his sound one full of new and painful kinks. Also, in honor of the occasion he had committed the error of wearing a pair of stiff and inflexible new shoes; wherefore he had worn his carpet slippers ever since.

Missing the fiftieth anniversary was not the main point with the corporal — that was merely the fortune of war, to be accepted with fortitude and with no more than a proper and natural amount of grumbling by one who had been a good soldier and was now a good citizen; but for days before the event, and daily ever since, divers members of the old regiment had been writing pieces to the papers — the German papers and the English-printing papers too — long pieces, telling of the trip to Washington, and then on into Virginia and Tennessee, speaking of this campaign and that and this battle and that. And because there was just now a passing wave of interest in Civil War matters, the papers had printed these contributions, thereby reflecting much glory on the writers thereof. But Corporal Speck, reading these things, had marveled deeply that sane men should have such disgustingly bad memories; for his own recollection of these stirring and epochal events differed most widely from the reminiscent narration of each misguided chronicler.

It was, indeed, a shameful thing that the most important occurrences of the whole war should be so shockingly mangled and mishandled in the retelling. They were so grievously wrong, those other veterans, and he was so absolutely right. He was always right in these matters. Only the night before, during a merciful respite from his nursing duties, he had, in Otto Wittenpen's back barroom, spoken across the rim of a tall stein with some bitterness of certain especially grievous misstatements of plain fact on the part of certain faulty-minded comrades. In reply Otto had said, in a rather sneering tone the corporal thought:

"Say, then, Jacob, why don't you yourself write a piece to the paper telling about this regiment of yours — the way it was?"

"I will. Tomorrow I will do so without fail," he had said, the ambition of authorship suddenly stirring within him. Now, however, as he sat at the kitchen window, he gloomed in his disappointment, for he had tried and he knew he had not the gift of the written line. A good soldier he had been — yes, none better — and a good citizen, and in his day a capable and painstaking doorkeeper in the tax office; but he could not write his own story. That morning, when the youngest grandchild slept and his daughter and his daughter's husband and the brood of his older grandchildren were all at the Lutheran church over in the next block, he sat himself down to compose his article to the paper; but the words would not come — or, at least, after the first line or two they would not come.

The mental pictures of those stirring great days when he marched off on his two good legs — both good legs then — to fight for the country whose language he could not yet speak was there in bright and living colors; but the sorry part of it was he could not clothe them in language. In the trash box under the sink a dozen crumpled sheets of paper testified to his failure, and now, alone with the youngest Miss Engel, he brooded over it and got low in his mind and let his pipe go smack out. And right then and there, with absolutely no warning at all, there came to him, as you might say from the clear sky, a great idea — an idea so magnificent that he almost dropped the youngest Miss Engel off his lap at the splendid shock of it.

With solicitude he glanced down at the small, moist, pink, lumpy bundle of prickly heat and sore gums. Despite the sudden jostle the young lady slept steadily on. Very carefully he laid his pipe aside and very carefully he got upon his feet, jouncing his charge soothingly up and down, and with deftness he committed her small person to the crib that stood handily by. She stirred fretfully, but did not wake. The corporal steered his gimpy leg and his rheumatic one out of the kitchen, which was white with scouring and as clean as a new pin, into the rearmost and smallest of the three sleeping rooms that mainly made up the Speck-Engel apartment.

The bed, whereon of nights Corporal Speck reposed with a bucking bronco of an eight-year-old grandson for a bedmate, was jammed close against the plastering, under the one small window set diagonally in a jog in the wall, and opening out upon an airshaft, like a chimney. Time had been when the corporal had a room and a bed all his own; that was before the family began to grow so fast in its second generation and while he still held a place of lucrative employment at the tax office.

As he got down upon his knees beside the bed the old man uttered a little groan of discomfort. He felt about in the space underneath and drew out a small tin trunk, rusted on its corners and dented in its sides. He made a laborious selection of keys from a key-ring he got out of his pocket, unlocked the trunk and lifted out a heavy top tray. The tray contained, among other things, such treasures as his naturalization papers, his pension papers, a photograph of his dead wife, and a small bethumbed passbook of the East Side Germania Savings Bank. Underneath was a black fatigue hat with a gold cord round its crown, a neatly folded blue uniform coat, with the G. A. R. bronze showing in its uppermost lapel, and below that, in turn, the suit of neat black the corporal wore on high state occasions and would one day wear to be buried in. Pawing and digging, he worked his hands to the very bottom, and then, with a little grunt, he heaved out the thing he wanted — the one trophy, except a stiffened kneecap and an honorable record, this old man had brought home from the South. It was a captured Confederate knapsack, flattened and flabby. Its leather was dry-rotted with age and the brass C. S. A. on the outer flap was gangrened and sunken in; the flap curled up stiffly, like an old shoe sole.

The crooked old fingers undid a buckle fastening and from the musty and odorous interior of the knapsack withdrew a letter, in a queer-looking yellowed envelope, with a queer-looking stamp upon the upper right-hand corner and a faint superscription upon its face. The three sheets of paper he slid out of the envelope were too old even to rustle, but the close writing upon them in a brownish, faded ink was still plainly to be made out.

Corporal Speck replaced the knapsack in its place at the very bottom, put the tray back in its place, closed the trunk and locked it and shoved it under the bed. The trunk resisted slightly and he lost one carpet slipper and considerable breath in the struggle. Limping back to the kitchen and seeing that little Miss Engel still slumbered, he eased his frame into a chair and composed himself to literary composition, not in the least disturbed by the shouts of roistering sidewalk comedians that filtered up to him from down below in front of the house, or by the distant clatter of intermittent traffic over the cobbly spine of Second Avenue, half a block away. For some time he wrote, with a most scratchy pen; and this is what he wrote:

"To the Editor of the Sun, City.

"*Dear Sir*: The undersigned would state that he served two years and nine months — until wounded in action — in the Fighting Two Hundred and Tenth New York Infantry, and has been much interested to see what other comrades wrote for the papers regarding same in connection with the Rebellion War of North and South respectively. I would state that during the battle of Chickamauga I was for a while lying near by to a Confederate soldier — name unknown — who was dying on account of a wound in the chest. By his request I gave him a drink of water from my canteen, he dying shortly thereafter. Being myself wounded — right knee shattered by a Minie ball — I was removed to a field hospital; but before doing so I brought away this man's knapsack for a keepsake of the occasion. Some years later I found in said knapsack a letter, which previous to then was overlooked by me. I inclose herewith a copy of said letter, which it may be interesting for reading purposes by surviving comrades.

"Respectfully yours,

"Jacob Speck,

"Late Corporal L Company,

"Fighting Two Hundred and Tenth New York, U. S. A."

With deliberation and squeaky emphasis the pen progressed slowly across the paper, while the corporal, with his left hand, held flat the dead man's ancient letter before him, intent on copying it. Hard words puzzled him and long words daunted him, and he was making a long job of it when there were steps in the hall without. There entered breezily Miss Hortense Engel, who was the oldest of all the multiplying Engels, pretty beyond question and every inch American, having the gift of wearing Lower Sixth Avenue stock designs in a way to make them seem Upper Fifth Avenue models. Miss Engel's face was pleasantly flushed; she had just parted lingeringly from her steady company, whose name was Mr. Lawrence J. McLaughlin, in the lower hallway, which is the trysting place and courting place of tenement-dwelling sweethearts, and now she had come to make ready the family's cold Sunday night tea. At sight of her the corporal had another inspiration — his second within the hour. His brow smoothed and he fetched a sigh of relief.

"'Lo, grosspops!" she said. "How's every little thing? The kiddo all right?"

She unpinned a Sunday hat that was plumed like a hearse and slipped on a long apron that covered her from Robespierre bib to hobble hem.

"Girl," said her grandfather, "would you make tomorrow for me at the office a copy of this letter on the typewriter machine?"

He spoke in German and she answered in New-Yorkese, while her nimble fingers wrestled with the task of back-buttoning her apron.

"Sure thing! It won't take hardly a minute to rattle that off. Funny-looking old thing!" she went on, taking up the creased and faded original. "Who wrote it? And whatcher goin' to do with it, grosspops?"

"That," he told her, "is mine own business! It is for you, please, to make the copy and bring both to me tomorrow, the letter and also the copy."

So on Monday morning, when the rush of taking dictation at the office of the Great American Hosiery Company, in Broome Street, was well abated, the competent Miss Hortense copied the letter, and that same evening her grandfather mailed it to the Sun, accompanied by his own introduction. The Sun straightway printed it without change and — what was still better — with the sender's name spelled out in capital letters; and that night, at the place down by the corner, Corporal Jacob Speck was a prophet not without honor in his own country — much honor, in fact, accrued.

If you have read certain other stories of mine you may remember that, upon a memorable occasion, Judge William Pitman Priest made a trip to New York and while there had dealings with a Mr. J. Hayden Witherbee, a promoter of gas and other hot-air propositions; and that during the course of his stay in the metropolis he made the acquaintance of one Malley, a Sun reporter. This had happened some years back, but Malley was still on the staff of the Sun. It happened also that, going through the paper to clip out and measure up his own space, Malley came upon the corporal's contribution. Glancing over it idly, he caught the name, twice or thrice repeated, of the town where Judge Priest lived. So he bundled together a couple of copies and sent them South with a short letter; and therefore it came about in due season, through the good offices of the United States Post-office Department, that these enclosures reached the judge on a showery afternoon as he loafed upon his wide front porch, waiting for his supper.

First, he read Malley's letter and was glad to hear from Malley. With a quickened interest he ran a plump thumb under the wrappings of the two close-rolled papers, opened out one of them at page ten and read the opening statement of Corporal Jacob Speck, for whom instantly the judge conceived a long-distance fondness. Next he came to the letter that Miss Hortense Engel had so accurately transcribed, and at the very first words of it he sat up straighter, with a surprised and gratified little grunt; for he had known them both — the writer of that letter and its recipient. One still lived in his memory as a red-haired girl with a pert, malicious face, and the other as a stripling youth in a ragged gray uniform. And he had known most of those whose names studded the printed lines so thickly. Indeed, some of them he still knew — only now they were old men and old women — faded, wrinkled bucks and belles of a far-distant day.

As he read the first words it came back to the judge, almost with the jolting emphasis of a new and fresh sensation, that in the days of his own youth he had never liked the girl who wrote that letter or the man who received it. But she was dead this many and many a year — why, she must have died soon after she wrote this very letter — the date proved that — and he, the man, had fallen at Chickamauga, taking his death in front like a soldier; and surely that settled everything and made all things right! But the letter — that was the main thing. His old blue eyes skipped nimbly behind the glasses that saddled the tip of his plump pink nose, and the old judge read it — just such a letter as he himself had received many a time; just such a wartime letter as uncounted thousands of soldiers North and South received from their sweethearts and read and reread by the light of flickering campfires and carried afterward in their knapsacks through weary miles of marching.

It was crammed with the small-town gossip of a small town that was but little more than a memory now — telling how, because he would not volunteer, a hapless youth had been waylaid by a dozen high-spirited girls and overpowered, and dressed in a woman's shawl and a woman's poke bonnet, so that he left town with his shame between two suns; how, since the Yankees had come, sundry faithless females were friendly — actually friendly, this being underscored — with the more personable of the young Yankee officers; how half the town was in mourning for a son or brother dead or wounded; how a new and sweetly sentimental song, called Rosalie, the Prairie Flower, was being much sung at the time — and had it reached the army yet? how old Mrs. Hobbs had been exiled to Canada for seditious acts and language and had departed northward between two files of bluecoats, reviling the Yankees with an unbitted tongue at every step; how So-and-So had died or married or gone refugeeing below the enemy's line into safely Southern territory; how this thing had happened and that thing had not.

The old judge read on and on, catching gladly at names that kindled a tenderly warm glow of half-forgotten memories in his soul, until he came to the last paragraph of all; and then, as he comprehended the intent of it in all its barbed and venomed malice, he stood suddenly erect, with the outspread paper shaking in his hard grip. For now, coming back to him by so strange a way across fifty years of silence and misunderstanding, he read there the answer to the town's oldest, biggest tragedy and knew what it was that all this time had festered, like buried thorns, in the flesh of those two men, his comrades and friends. He dropped the paper, and up and down the wide, empty porch he stumped on his short stout legs, shaking with the shock of revelation and with indignation and pity for the blind and bitter uselessness of it all.

"Ah hah!" he said to himself over and over again understandingly. "Ah hah!" And then: "Next to a mean man, a mean woman is the meanest thing in this whole created world, I reckin. I ain't sure but what she's the meanest of the two. And to think of what them two did between 'em — she writin' that hellish black lyin' tale to 'Lonzo Pike and he puttin' off hotfoot to Abner Tilghman to poison his mind with it and set him like a flint against his own flesh and blood! And wasn't it jest like Lon Pike to go and git himself killed the next day after he got that there letter! And wasn't it jest like her to up and die before the truth could be brought home to her! And wasn't it like them two stubborn, set, contrary, close-mouthed Tilghman boys to go 'long through all these years, without neither one of 'em ever offerin' to make or take an explanation!" His tone changed. "Oh, ain't it been a pitiful thing! And all so useless! But — oh, thank the Lord — it ain't too late to mend it part way anyhow! Thank God, it ain't too late for that!"

Exulting now, he caught up the paper he had dropped, and with it crumpled in his pudgy fist was half-way down the gravel walk, bound for the little cottage snuggled in its vine ambush across Clay Street before a better and a bigger inspiration caught up with him and halted him midway of an onward stride.

Was not this the second Friday in the month? It certainly was. And would not the Camp be meeting tonight in regular semimonthly session at Kamleiter's Hall? It certainly would. For just a moment Judge Priest considered the proposition. He slapped his linen clad flank gleefully, and his round old face, which had been knotted with resolution, broke up into a wrinkly, ample smile; he spun on his heel and hurried back into the house and to the telephone in the hall. For half an hour, more or less, Judge Priest was busy at that telephone, calling in a high, excited voice, first for one number and then for another. While he did this his supper grew cold on the table, and in the dining room Jeff, the white-clad, fidgeted and out in the kitchen Aunt Dilsey, the turbaned, fumed — but, at Kamleiter's Hall that night at eight, Judge Priest's industry was in abundant fulness rewarded.

Once upon a time Gideon K. Irons Camp claimed a full two hundred members, but that had been when it was first organized. Now there were in good standing less than twenty. Of these twenty, fifteen sat on the hard wooden chairs when Judge Priest rapped with his metal spectacle case for order, and that fifteen meant all who could travel out at nights. Doctor Lake was there, and Sergeant Jimmy Bagby, the faithful and inevitable. It was the biggest turnout the Camp had had in a year.

Far over on one side, cramped down in a chair, was Captain Abner Tilghman, feeble and worn-looking. His buggy horse stood hitched by the curb downstairs. Sergeant Jimmy Bagby had gone to his house for him and on the plea of business of vital moment had made him come with him. Almost directly across the middle aisle on the other side sat Mr. Edward Tilghman. Nobody had to go for him. He always came to a regular meeting of the Camp, even though he heard the proceedings only in broken bits.

The adjutant called the roll and those present answered, each one to his name; and mainly the voices sounded bent and sagged, like the bodies of their owners. A keen onlooker might have noticed a sort of tremulous, joyous impatience, which filled all save two of these old, gray men, pushing the preliminaries forward with uncommon speed. They fidgeted in their places.

Presently Judge Priest cleared his throat of a persistent huskiness and stood up.

"Before we proceed to the regular routine," he piped, "I desire to present a certain matter to a couple of our members." He came down off the little platform, where the flags were draped, with a step that was almost light, and into Captain Abner Tilghman's hand he put a copy of a city paper, turned and folded at a certain place, where a column of printed matter was scored about with heavy pencil bracketings. "Cap'n," he said, "as a personal favor to me, suh, would you please read this here article? — the one that's marked" — he pointed with his finger — "not aloud — read it to yourself, please."

It was characteristic of the paralytic to say nothing. Without a word he adjusted his glasses and without a word he began to read. So instantly intent was he that he did not see what followed next — and that was Judge Priest crossing over to Mr. Edward Tilghman's side with another copy of a paper in his hand.

"Ed," he bade him, "read this here article, won't you? Read it clear through to the end — it might interest you maybe." The deaf man looked up at him wonderingly, but took the paper in his slightly palsied hand and bent his head close above the printed sheet.

Judge Priest stood in the middle aisle, making no move to go back to his own place. He watched the two silent readers. All the others watched them too. They read on, making slow progress, for the light was poor and their eyes were poor. And the watchers could hardly contain themselves; they could hardly wait. Sergeant Jimmy Bagby kept bobbing up and down like a pudgy jack-in-the-box that is slightly stiff in its joints. A small, restrained rustle of bodies accompanied the rustle of the folded newspapers held in shaky hands.

Unconscious of all scrutiny, the brothers read on. Perhaps because he had started first — perhaps because his glasses were the more expensive and presumably therefore the more helpful — Captain Abner Tilghman came to the concluding paragraph first. He read it through — and then Judge Priest turned his head away, for a moment almost regretting he had chosen so public a place for this thing.

He looked back again in time to see Captain Abner getting upon his feet. Dragging his dead leg behind him, the paralytic crossed the bare floor to where his brother's gray head was bent to his task. And at his side he halted, making no sound or sign, but only waiting. He waited there, trembling all over, until the sitter came to the end of the column and read what was there — and lifted a face all glorified with a perfect understanding.

"Eddie!" said the older man — "Eddie!" He uttered a name of boyhood affection that none there had heard uttered for fifty years nearly; and it was as though a stone had been rolled away from a tomb — as though out of the grave of a dead past a voice had been resurrected. "Eddie!"

he said a third time, pleadingly, abjectly, humbly, craving for forgiveness.

"Brother Abner!" said the other man. "Oh, Brother Abner!" he said — and that was all he did say — all he had need to say, for he was on his feet now, reaching out with wide-spread, shaking arms.

Sergeant Jimmy Bagby tried to start a cheer, but could not make it come out of his throat — only a clicking, squeaking kind of sound came. As a cheer it was a miserable failure.

Side by side, each with his inner arm tight gripped about the other, the brothers, bareheaded, turned their backs upon their friends and went away. Slowly they passed out through the doorway into the darkness of the stair landing, and the members of the Gideon K. Irons Camp were all up on their feet.

"Mind that top step, Abner!" they heard the younger man say. "Wait! I'll help you down."

That was all that was heard, except a scuffling sound of uncertainly placed feet, growing fainter and fainter as the two brothers passed down the long stairs of Kamleiter's Hall and out into the night — that was all, unless you would care to take cognizance of a subdued little chorus such as might be produced by twelve or thirteen elderly men snuffling in a large bare room. As commandant of the Camp it was fitting, perhaps, that Judge Priest should speak first.

"The trouble with this here Camp is jest this," he said: "it's got a lot of snifflin' old fools in it that don't know no better than to bust out cryin' when they oughter be happy!" And then, as if to show how deeply he felt the shame of such weakness on the part of others, Judge Priest blew his nose with great violence, and for a space of minutes industriously mopped at his indignant eyes with an enormous pocket handkerchief.

In accordance with a rule, Jeff Poindexter waited up for his employer. Jeff expected him by nine-thirty at the latest; but it was actually getting along toward ten-thirty before Jeff, who had been dozing lightly in the dim-lit hall, oblivious to the fanged attentions of some large mosquitoes, roused suddenly as he heard the sound of a rambling but familiar step clunking along the wooden sidewalk of Clay Street. The latch on the front gate clicked, and as Jeff poked his nose out of the front door he heard, down the aisle of trees that bordered the gravel walk, the voice of his master uplifted in solitary song.

In the matter of song the judge had a peculiarity. It made no difference what the words might be or the theme — he sang every song and all songs to a fine, high, tuneless little tune of his own. At this moment Judge Priest, as Jeff gathered, was showing a wide range of selection. One second he was announcing that his name it was Joe Bowers and he was all the way from Pike, and the next he was stating, for the benefit of all who might care to hear these details, that they — presumably certain horses — were bound to run all night — bound to run all day; so you could bet on the bobtailed nag and he'd bet on the bay. Nearer to the porch steps it boastingly transpired that somebody had jumped aboard the telegraf and steered her by the triggers, whereat the lightnin' flew and 'lectrified and killed ten thousand niggers! But even so general a catastrophe could not weigh down the singer's spirits. As he put a fumbling foot upon the lowermost step of the porch, he threw his head far back and shrilly issued the following blanket invitation to ladies resident in a far-away district:

Oh, Bowery gals, won't you come out tonight?Won't you come out tonight?Oh, Bowery gals, won't you come out tonight,And dance by the light of the moon?I danced with a gal with a hole in her stockin';And her heel it kep' a-rockin' — kep' a-rockin'!She was the purtiest gal in the room!

Jeff pulled the front door wide open. The song stopped and Judge Priest stood in the opening, teetering a little on his heels. His face was all a blushing pinky glow.

"Evenin', jedge!" greeted Jeff. "You're late, suh!"

"Jeff," said Judge Priest slowly, "it's a beautiful evenin'."

Amazed, Jeff stared at him. As a matter of fact, the drizzle of the afternoon had changed, soon after dark, to a steady downpour. The judge's limpened hat brim dripped raindrops and his shoulders were sopping wet, but Jeff had yet to knowingly and wilfully contradict a prominent white citizen.

"Yas, suh!" he said, half affirmatively, half questioningly. "Is it?"

"It is so!" said Judge Priest. "Every star in the sky shines like a diamond! Jeff, it's the most beautiful evenin' I ever remember!"

VIII

FISHHEAD

It goes past the powers of my pen to try to describe Reelfoot Lake for you so that you, reading this, will get the picture of it in your mind as I have it in mine. For Reelfoot Lake is like no other lake that I know anything about. It is an afterthought of Creation.

The rest of this continent was made and had dried in the sun for thousands of years — for millions of years for all I know — before Reelfoot came to be. It's the newest big thing in nature on this hemisphere probably, for it was formed by the great earthquake of 1811, just a little more than a hundred years ago. That earthquake of 1811 surely altered the face of the earth on the then far frontier of this country. It changed the course of rivers, it converted hills into what are now the sunk lands of three states, and it turned the solid ground to jelly and made it roll in waves like the sea. And in the midst of the retching of the land and the vomiting of the waters it depressed to varying depths a section of the earth crust sixty miles long, taking it down — trees, hills, hollows and all; and a crack broke through to the Mississippi River so that for three days the river ran up stream, filling the hole.

The result was the largest lake south of the Ohio, lying mostly in Tennessee, but extending up across what is now the Kentucky line, and taking its name from a fancied resemblance in its outline to the splay, reeled foot of a cornfield negro. Niggerwool Swamp, not so far away, may have got its name from the same man who christened Reelfoot; at least so it sounds.

Reelfoot is, and has always been, a lake of mystery. In places it is bottomless. Other places the skeletons of the cypress trees that went down when the earth sank still stand upright, so that if the sun shines from the right quarter and the water is less muddy than common, a man peering face downward into its depths sees, or thinks he sees, down below him the bare top-limbs upstretching like drowned men's fingers, all coated with the mud of years and bandaged with pennons of the green lake slime. In still other places the lake is shallow for long stretches, no deeper than breast deep to a man, but dangerous because of the weed growths and the sunken drifts which entangle a swimmer's limbs. Its banks are mainly mud, its waters are muddied too, being a rich coffee color in the spring and a copperish yellow in the summer, and the trees along its shore are mud colored clear up to their lower limbs after the spring floods, when the dried sediment covers their trunks with a thick, scrofulous-looking coat.

There are stretches of unbroken woodland around it and slashes where the cypress knees rise countlessly like headstones and footstones for the dead snags that rot in the soft ooze. There are deadenings with the lowland corn growing high and rank below and the bleached, fire-blackened girdled trees rising above, barren of leaf and limb. There are long, dismal flats where in the spring the clotted frog-spawn clings like patches of white mucus among the weed stalks and at night the turtles crawl out to lay clutches of perfectly round, white eggs with tough, rubbery shells in the sand. There are bayous leading off to nowhere and sloughs that wind aimlessly, like great, blind worms, to finally join the big river that rolls its semi-liquid torrents a few miles to the westward.

So Reelfoot lies there, flat in the bottoms, freezing lightly in the winter, steaming torridly in the summer, swollen in the spring when the woods have turned a vivid green and the buffalo gnats by the million and the billion fill the flooded hollows with their pestilential buzzing, and in the fall ringed about gloriously with all the colors which the first frost brings — gold of hickory, yellow-russet of sycamore, red of dogwood and ash and purple-black of sweet-gum.

But the Reelfoot country has its uses. It is the best game and fish country, natural or artificial, that is left in the South today. In their appointed seasons the duck and the geese flock in, and even semi-tropical birds, like the brown pelican and the Florida snake-bird, have been known to come there to nest. Pigs, gone back to wildness, range the ridges, each razor-backed drove captained by a gaunt, savage, slab-sided old boar. By night the bull frogs, inconceivably big and tremendously vocal, bellow under the banks.

It is a wonderful place for fish — bass and crappie and perch and the snouted buffalo fish. How these edible sorts live to spawn and how their spawn in turn live to spawn again is a marvel, seeing how many of the big fish-eating cannibal fish there are in Reelfoot. Here, bigger than anywhere else, you find the garfish, all bones and appetite and horny plates, with a snout like an alligator, the nearest link, naturalists say, between the animal life of today and the animal life of the Reptilian Period. The shovel-nose cat, really a deformed kind of freshwater sturgeon, with a great fan-shaped membranous plate jutting out from his nose like a bowsprit, jumps all day in the quiet places with mighty splashing sounds, as though a horse had fallen into the water. On every stranded log the huge snapping turtles lie on sunny days in groups of four and six, baking their shells black in the sun, with their little snaky heads raised watchfully, ready to slip noiselessly off at the first sound of oars grating in the row-locks.

But the biggest of them all are the catfish. These are monstrous creatures, these catfish of Reelfoot — scaleless, slick things, with corpsy, dead eyes and poisonous fins like javelins and long whiskers dangling from the sides of their cavernous heads. Six and seven feet long they grow to be and to weigh two hundred pounds or more, and they have mouths wide enough to take in a man's foot or a man's fist and strong enough to break any hook save the strongest and greedy enough to eat anything, living or dead or putrid, that the horny jaws can master. Oh, but they are wicked things, and they tell wicked tales of them down there. They call them man-eaters and compare them, in certain of their habits, to sharks.

Fishhead was of a piece with this setting. He fitted into it as an acorn fits its cup. All his life he had lived on Reelfoot, always in the one place, at the mouth of a certain slough. He had been born there, of a negro father and a half-breed Indian mother, both of them now dead, and the story was that before his birth his mother was frightened by one of the big fish, so that the child came into the world most hideously marked. Anyhow, Fishhead was a human monstrosity, the veritable embodiment of nightmare. He had the body of a man — a short, stocky, sinewy body — but his face was as near to being the face of a great fish as any face could be and yet retain some trace of human aspect. His skull sloped back so abruptly that he could hardly be said to have a forehead at all; his chin slanted off right into nothing. His eyes were small and round with shallow, glazed, pale-yellow pupils, and they were set wide apart in his head and they were unwinking and staring, like a fish's eyes. His nose was no more than a pair of tiny slits in the middle of the yellow mask. His mouth was the worst of all. It was the awful mouth of a catfish, lipless and almost inconceivably wide, stretching from side to side. Also when Fishhead became a man grown his likeness to a fish increased, for the hair upon his face grew out into two tightly kinked, slender pendants that drooped down either side of the mouth like the beards of a fish.

If he had any other name than Fishhead, none excepting he knew it. As Fishhead he was known and as Fishhead he answered. Because he knew the waters and the woods of

Reelfoot better than any other man there, he was valued as a guide by the city men who came every year to hunt or fish; but there were few such jobs that Fishhead would take. Mainly he kept to himself, tending his corn patch, netting the lake, trapping a little and in season pot hunting for the city markets. His neighbors, ague-bitten whites and malaria-proof negroes alike, left him to himself. Indeed for the most part they had a superstitious fear of him. So he lived alone, with no kith nor kin, nor even a friend, shunning his kind and shunned by them.

His cabin stood just below the state line, where Mud Slough runs into the lake. It was a shack of logs, the only human habitation for four miles up or down. Behind it the thick timber came shouldering right up to the edge of Fishhead's small truck patch, enclosing it in thick shade except when the sun stood just overhead. He cooked his food in a primitive fashion, outdoors, over a hole in the soggy earth or upon the rusted red ruin of an old cook stove, and he drank the saffron water of the lake out of a dipper made of a gourd, faring and fending for himself, a master hand at skiff and net, competent with duck gun and fish spear, yet a creature of affliction and loneliness, part savage, almost amphibious, set apart from his fellows, silent and suspicious.

In front of his cabin jutted out a long fallen cottonwood trunk, lying half in and half out of the water, its top side burnt by the sun and worn by the friction of Fishhead's bare feet until it showed countless patterns of tiny scrolled lines, its under side black and rotted and lapped at unceasingly by little waves like tiny licking tongues. Its farther end reached deep water. And it was a part of Fishhead, for no matter how far his fishing and trapping might take him in the daytime, sunset would find him back there, his boat drawn up on the bank and he on the outer end of this log. From a distance men had seen him there many times, sometimes squatted, motionless as the big turtles that would crawl upon its dipping tip in his absence, sometimes erect and vigilant like a creek crane, his misshapen yellow form outlined against the yellow sun, the yellow water, the yellow banks — all of them yellow together.

If the Reelfooters shunned Fishhead by day they feared him by night and avoided him as a plague, dreading even the chance of a casual meeting. For there were ugly stories about Fishhead — stories which all the negroes and some of the whites believed. They said that a cry which had been heard just before dusk and just after, skittering across the darkened waters, was his calling cry to the big cats, and at his bidding they came trooping in, and that in their company he swam in the lake on moonlight nights, sporting with them, diving with them, even feeding with them on what manner of unclean things they fed. The cry had been heard many times, that much was certain, and it was certain also that the big fish were noticeably thick at the mouth of Fishhead's slough. No native Reelfooter, white or black, would willingly wet a leg or an arm there.

Here Fishhead had lived and here he was going to die. The Baxters were going to kill him, and this day in midsummer was to be the time of the killing. The two Baxters — Jake and Joel — were coming in their dugout to do it. This murder had been a long time in the making. The Baxters had to brew their hate over a slow fire for months before it reached the pitch of action. They were poor whites, poor in everything — repute and worldly goods and standing — a pair of fever-ridden squatters who lived on whisky and tobacco when they could get it, and on fish and cornbread when they couldn't.

The feud itself was of months' standing. Meeting Fishhead one day in the spring on the spindly scaffolding of the skiff landing at Walnut Log, and being themselves far overtaken in liquor and vainglorious with a bogus alcoholic substitute for courage, the brothers had accused him, wantonly and without proof, of running their trot-line and stripping it of the hooked catch — an unforgivable sin among the water dwellers and the shanty boaters of the South. Seeing that he bore this accusation in silence, only eyeing them steadfastly, they had been emboldened then to slap his face, whereupon he turned and gave them both the beating of their lives — bloodying their noses and bruising their lips with hard blows against their front teeth, and finally leaving them, mauled and prone, in the dirt. Moreover, in the onlookers a sense of the everlasting fitness of things had triumphed over race prejudice and allowed them — two freeborn, sovereign whites — to be licked by a nigger.

Therefore, they were going to get the nigger. The whole thing had been planned out amply. They were going to kill him on his log at sundown. There would be no witnesses to see it, no retribution to follow after it. The very ease of the undertaking made them forget even their inborn fear of the place of Fishhead's habitation.

For more than an hour now they had been coming from their shack across a deeply indented arm of the lake. Their dugout, fashioned by fire and adz and draw-knife from the bole of a gum tree, moved through the water as noiselessly as a swimming mallard, leaving behind it a long, wavy trail on the stilled waters. Jake, the better oarsman sat flat in the stern of the round-bottomed craft, paddling with quick, splashless strokes. Joel, the better shot, was squatted forward. There was a heavy, rusted duck gun between his knees.

Though their spying upon the victim had made them certain sure he would not be about the shore for hours, a doubled sense of caution led them to hug closely the weedy banks. They slid along the shore like shadows, moving so swiftly and in such silence that the watchful mud turtles barely turned their snaky heads as they passed. So, a full hour before the time, they came slipping around the mouth of the slough and made for a natural ambuscade which the mixed breed had left within a stone's jerk of his cabin to his own undoing.

Where the slough's flow joined deeper water a partly uprooted tree was stretched, prone from shore, at the top still thick and green with leaves that drew nourishment from the earth in which the half-uncovered roots yet held, and twined about with an exuberance of trumpet vines and wild fox-grapes. All about was a huddle of drift — last year's cornstalks, shreddy strips of bark, chunks of rotted weed, all the riffle and dunnage of a quiet eddy. Straight into this green clump glided the dugout and swung, broadside on, against the protecting trunk of the tree, hidden from the inner side by the intervening curtains of rank growth, just as the Baxters had intended it should be hidden, when days before in their scouting they marked this masked place of waiting and included it, then and there, in the scope of their plans.

There had been no hitch or mishap. No one had been abroad in the late afternoon to mark their movements — and in a little while Fishhead ought to be due. Jake's woodman's eye followed the downward swing of the sun speculatively. The shadows, thrown shoreward, lengthened and slithered on the small ripples. The small noises of the day died out; the small noises of the coming night began to multiply. The green-bodied flies went away and big mosquitoes, with speckled gray legs, came to take the places of the flies. The sleepy lake sucked at the mud banks with small mouthing sounds as though it found the taste of the raw mud agreeable. A monster crawfish, big as a chicken lobster, crawled out of the top of his dried mud chimney and perched himself there, an armored sentinel on the watchtower. Bull bats began to flitter back and forth above the tops of the trees. A pudgy muskrat, swimming with head up, was moved to sidle off briskly as he met a cotton-mouth moccasin snake, so fat and swollen with summer poison that it looked almost like a legless lizard as it moved along the surface of the water in a series of slow torpid s's. Directly above the head of either of the waiting assassins a compact little swarm of midges hung, holding to a sort of kite-shaped formation.

A little more time passed and Fishhead came out of the woods at the back, walking swiftly, with a sack over his shoulder. For a few seconds his deformities showed in the clearing, then the black inside of the cabin swallowed him up. By now the sun was almost down. Only the red nub of it showed above the timber line across the lake, and the shadows lay inland a long way. Out beyond, the big cats were stirring, and the great smacking sounds as their twisting bodies leaped clear and fell back in the water came shoreward in a chorus.

But the two brothers in their green covert gave heed to nothing except the one thing upon which their hearts were set and their nerves tensed. Joel gently shoved his gun-barrels across the log, cuddling the stock to his shoulder and slipping two fingers caressingly back and forth upon the triggers. Jake held the narrow dugout steady by a grip upon a fox-grape tendril.

A little wait and then the finish came. Fishhead emerged from the cabin door and came down the narrow footpath to the water and out upon the water on his log. He was barefooted and bareheaded, his cotton shirt open down the front to show his yellow neck and breast, his dungaree trousers held about his waist by a twisted tow string. His broad splay feet, with the prehensile toes outspread, gripped the polished curve of the log as he moved along its swaying, dipping surface until he came to its outer end and stood there erect, his chest filling, his chinless face lifted up and something of mastership and dominion in his poise. And then — his eye caught what another's eyes might have missed — the round, twin ends of the gun barrels, the fixed gleams of Joel's eyes, aimed at him through the green tracery.

In that swift passage of time, too swift almost to be measured by seconds, realization flashed all through him, and he threw his head still higher and opened wide his shapeless trap of a mouth, and out across the lake he sent skittering and rolling his cry. And in his cry was the laugh of a loon, and the croaking bellow of a frog, and the bay of a hound, all the compounded night noises of the lake. And in it, too, was a farewell and a defiance and an appeal. The heavy roar of the duck gun came.

At twenty yards the double charge tore the throat out of him. He came down, face forward, upon the log and clung there, his trunk twisting distortedly, his legs twitching and kicking like the legs of a speared frog, his shoulders hunching and lifting spasmodically as the life ran out of him all in one swift coursing flow. His head canted up between the heaving shoulders, his eyes looked full on the staring face of his murderer, and then the blood came out of his mouth and Fishhead, in death still as much fish as man, slid flopping, head first, off the end of the log and sank, face downward, slowly, his limbs all extended out. One after another a string of big bubbles came up to burst in the middle of a widening reddish stain on the coffee-colored water.

The brothers watched this, held by the horror of the thing they had done, and the cranky dugout, tipped far over by the recoil of the gun, took water steadily across its gunwale; and now there was a sudden stroke from below upon its careening bottom and it went over and they were in the lake. But shore was only twenty feet away, the trunk of the uprooted tree only five. Joel, still holding fast to his hot gun, made for the log, gaining it with one stroke. He threw his free arm over it and clung there, treading water, as he shook his eyes free. Something gripped him — some great, sinewy, unseen thing gripped him fast by the thigh, crushing down on his flesh.

He uttered no cry, but his eyes popped out and his mouth set in a square shape of agony, and his fingers gripped into the bark of the tree like grapples. He was pulled down and down, by steady jerks, not rapidly but steadily, so steadily, and as he went his fingernails tore four little white strips in the tree bark. His mouth went under, next his popping eyes, then his erect hair, and finally his clawing, clutching hand, and that was the end of him.

Jake's fate was harder still, for he lived longer — long enough to see Joel's finish. He saw it through the water that ran down his face, and with a great surge of his whole body he literally flung himself across the log and jerked his legs up high into the air to save them. He flung himself too far, though, for his face and chest hit the water on the far side. And out of this water rose the head of a great fish, with the lake slime of years on its flat, black head, its whiskers bristling, its corpsy eyes alight. Its horny jaws closed and clamped in the front of Jake's flannel shirt. His hand struck out wildly and was speared on a poisoned fin, and unlike Joel, he went from sight with a great yell and a whirling and a churning of the water that made the cornstalks circle on the edges of a small whirlpool.

But the whirlpool soon thinned away into widening rings of ripples and the cornstalks quit circling and became still again, and only the multiplying night noises sounded about the mouth of the slough.

The bodies of all three came ashore on the same day near the same place. Except for the gaping gunshot wound where the neck met the chest, Fishhead's body was unmarked. But the bodies of the two Baxters were so marred and mauled that the Reelfooters buried them together on the bank without ever knowing which might be Jake's and which might be Joel's.

IX
GUILTY AS CHARGED

The Jew, I take it, is essentially temperamental, whereas the Irishman is by nature sentimental; so that in the long run both of them may reach the same results by varying mental routes. This, however, has nothing to do with the story I am telling here, except inferentially.

It was trial day at headquarters. To be exact, it was the tail end of trial day at headquarters. The mills of the police gods, which grind not so slowly but ofttimes exceeding fine, were about done with their grinding; and as the last of the grist came through the hopper, the last of the afternoon sunlight came sifting in through the windows at the west, thin and pale as skim milk. One after another the culprits, patrolmen mainly, had been arraigned on charges preferred by a superior officer, who was usually a lieutenant or a captain, but once in a while an inspector, full-breasted and gold-banded, like a fat blue bumblebee. In due turn each offender had made his defense; those who were lying about it did their lying, as a rule, glibly and easily and with a certain bogus frankness very pleasing to see. Contrary to a general opinion, the Father of Lies is often quite good to his children. But those who were telling the truth were frequently shamefaced and mumbling of speech, making poor impressions.

In due turn, also, each man had been convicted or had been acquitted, yet all — the proven innocent and the adjudged guilty alike — had undergone punishment, since they all had to sit and listen to lectures on police discipline and police manners from the trial deputy. It was perhaps as well for the peace and good order of the community that the public did not attend these séances. Those classes now that are the most thoroughly and most personally governed — the pushcart pedlers, with the permanent cringing droops in their alien backs; the sinful small boys, who play baseball in the streets against the statutes made and provided; the broken old wrecks, who ambush the prosperous passer-by in the shadows of dark corners, begging for money with which to keep body and soul together — it was just as well perhaps that none of them was admitted there to see these large, firm, stern men in uniform wriggling on the punishment chair, fumbling at their buttons, explaining, whining, even begging for mercy under the lashing flail of Third Deputy Commissioner Donohue's sleety judgments.

"The only time old Donny warms up is when he's got a grudge against you," a wit of headquarters — Larry Magee by name — had said once as he came forth from the ordeal, brushing imaginary hailstones off his shoulders. "It's always snowing hard in his soul!"

Unlike most icy-tempered men, though, Third Deputy Commissioner Donohue was addicted to speech. Dearly he loved to hear the sound of his own voice. Give to Donohue a congenial topic, such as some one's official or personal shortcomings, and a congenial audience, and he excelled mightily in saw-edged oratory, rolling his r's until the tortured consonants fairly lay on their backs and begged for mercy.

This, however, would have to be said for Deputy Commissioner Donohue — he was a hard one to fool. Himself a grayed ex-private of the force, who had climbed from the ranks step by step through slow and devious stages, he was coldly aware of every trick and device of the delinquent policeman. A new and particularly ingenious subterfuge, one that tasted of the fresh paint, might win his begrudged admiration — his gray flints of eyes would strike off sparks of grim appreciation; but then, nearly always, as though to discourage originality even in lying, he would plaster on the penalty — and the lecture — twice as thick. Wherefore, because of all these things, the newspaper men at headquarters viewed this elderly disciplinarian with mixed professional emotions. Presiding over a trial day, he made abundant copy for them, which was very good; but if the case were an important one he often prolonged it until they missed getting the result into their final editions, which, if you know anything about final editions, was very, very bad.

It was so on this particular afternoon. Here it was nearly dusk. The windows toward the east showed merely as opaque patches set against a wall of thickening gloom, and the third deputy commissioner had started in at two-thirty and was not done yet. Sparse and bony, he crouched forward on the edge of his chair, with his lean head drawn down between his leaner shoulders and his stiff stubble of hair erect on his scalp, and he looked, perching there, like a broody but vigilant old crested cormorant upon a barren rock.

Except for one lone figure of misery, the anxious bench below him was by now empty. Most of the witnesses were gone and most of the spectators, and all the newspaper men but two. He whetted a lean and crooked forefinger like a talon on the edge of the docket book, turned the page and called the last case, being the case of Patrolman James J. Rogan. Patrolman Rogan was a short horse and soon curried. For being on such and such a day, at such and such an hour, off his post, where he belonged, and in a saloon where he did not belong, sitting down, with his blouse unfastened and his belt unbuckled; and for having no better excuse, or no worse one, than the ancient tale of a sudden attack of faintness causing him to make his way into the nearest place where he might recover himself — that it happened to be a family liquor store was, he protested, a sheer accident — Patrolman Rogan was required to pay five days' pay and, moreover, to listen to divers remarks in which he heard himself likened to several things, none of them of a complimentary character.

Properly crushed and shrunken, the culprit departed thence with his uniform bagged and wrinkling upon his diminished form, and the third deputy commissioner, well pleased, on the whole, with his day's hunting, prepared to adjourn. The two lone reporters got up and made for the door, intending to telephone in to their two shops the grand total and final summary of old Donohue's bag of game.

They were at the door, in a little press of departing witnesses and late defendants, when behind them a word in Donohue's hard-rolled official accents made them halt and turn round. The veteran had picked up from his desk a sheet of paper and was squinting up his hedgy, thick eyebrows in an effort to read what was written there.

"Wan more case to be heard," he announced. "Keep order there, you men at the door! The case of Lieutenant Isidore Weil" — he grated the name out lingeringly — "charged with — with —" He broke off, peering about him for some one to scold. "Couldn't you be makin' a light here, some of you! I can't see to make out these here charges and specifications."

Some one bestirred himself and many lights popped on, chasing the shadows back into the far corners. Outside in the hall a policeman doing duty as a bailiff called the name of Lieutenant Isidore Weil, thrice repeated.

"Gee! Have they landed that slick kike at last?" said La Farge, the older of the reporters, half to himself. "Say, you know, that tickles me! I've been looking this long time for something like this to be coming off." Like most old headquarters reporters, La Farge had his deep-seated prejudices. To judge by his present expression, this was a very deep-seated one, amounting, you might say, to a constitutional infirmity with La Farge.

"Who's Weil and what's he done?" inquired Rogers. Rogers was a young reporter.

"I don't know yet — the charge must be newly filed, I guess," said La Farge, answering the last question first. "But I hope they nail him! I don't like him — never did. He's too fresh. He's too smart — one of those self-educated East Side Yiddishers, you know. Used to be a court interpreter down at Essex Market — knows about steen languages. And he — here he comes now."

Weil passed them, going into the trial room — a short, squarely built man with oily black hair above a dark, round face. Instantly you knew him for one of the effusive Semitic type; every angle and turn of his outward aspect testified frankly of his breed and his sort. And at sight of him entering you could almost see the gorge of Deputy Commissioner Donohue's race antagonism rising inside of him. His gray hackles stiffened and his thick-set eyebrows bristled outward like bits of frosted privet. Again he began whetting his forefinger on the leather back of the closed docket book. It was generally a bad sign for somebody when Donohue whetted his forefinger like that, and La Farge would have delighted to note it. But La Farge's appraising eyes were upon the accused.

"Listen!" he said under his breath to Rogers. "I think they must have the goods on Mister Wisenheimer at last. Usually he's the cockiest person round this building. Now take a look at him."

Indeed, there was a visible air of self-abasement about Lieutenant Weil as he crossed the wide chamber. It was a thing hard to define in words; yet undeniably there was a diffidence and a reluctance manifest in him, as though a sense of guilt wrestled with the man's natural conceit and assurance.

"Rogers," said La Farge, "let's hustle out and 'phone in what we've got and then come back right away. If this fellow's going to get the harpoon stuck into him I want to be on hand when he starts bleeding."

Only a few of the dwindled crowd turned back to hear the beginning of the case, whatever it might be, against the Jew. The rest scattered through the corridors, heading mainly for the exits, so that the two newspaper men had company as they hurried toward the main door, making for their offices across the street. When they came back the long cross halls were almost deserted; it had taken them a little longer to finish the job of telephoning than they had figured. At the door of the trial room stood one bulky blue figure. It was the acting bailiff.

"How far along have they got?" asked La Farge as the policeman made way for them to pass in.

"Captain Meagher is the first witness," said the policeman. "He's the one that's makin' the charge."

"What is the charge?" put in Rogers.

"At this distance I couldn't make out — Cap Meagher, he mumbles so," confessed the doorkeeper. "Somethin' about misuse of police property, I take it to be."

"Aha!" gloated La Farge in his gratification. "Come on, Rogers — I don't want to miss any of this."

It was plain, however, that they had missed something; for, to judge by his attitude, Captain Meagher was quite through with his testimony. He still sat in the witness chair alongside the deputy commissioner's desk; but he was silent and he stared vacantly at vacancy. Captain Meagher was known in the department as a man incredibly honest and unbelievably dull. He had no more imagination than one of his own reports. He had a long, sad face, like a tired workhorse's, and heavy black eyebrows that curved high in the middle and arched downward at each end — circumflexes accenting the incurable stupidity of his expression. His black mustache drooped the same way, too, in the design of an inverted magnet. Larry Magee had coined one of his best whimsies on the subject of the shape of the captain's mustache.

"No wonder," he said, "old Meagher never has any luck — he wears his horseshoe upside down on his face!"

Just as the two reporters, re-entering, took their seats the trial deputy spoke.

"Is that all, Captain Meagher?" he asked sonorously.

"That's all," said Meagher.

"I note," went on Donohue, glancing about him, "that the accused does not appear to be represented by counsel."

A man on trial at headquarters has the right to hire a lawyer to defend him.

"No, sir," spoke up Weil briskly. "I've got no lawyer, commissioner." His speech was the elaborated and painfully emphasized English of the self-taught East Sider. It carried in it just the bare suggestion of the racial lisp, and it made an acute contrast to the menacing Hibernian purr of Donohue's heavier voice. "I kind of thought I'd conduct my own case myself."

Donohue merely grunted.

"Do you desire, Lieutenant Weil, for to ask Captain Meagher any questions?" he demanded.

Weil shook his oily head of hair.

"No, sir. I wouldn't wish to ask the captain anything."

"Are there any other witnesses?" inquired Donohue next.

There was no answer. Plainly there were no other witnesses.

"Lieutenant Weil, do you desire for to say something in your own behalf?" queried the deputy commissioner.

"I think I'd like to," answered Weil.

He stood to be sworn, took the chair Meagher vacated and sat facing the room, appearing — so La Farge thought — more shamefaced and abashed than ever.

"Now, then," commanded Donohue impressively, "what statement, if any, have you to make, Lieutenant Weil, touchin' on this here charge preferred by your superior officer?"

Weil cleared his throat. Rogers figured that this bespoke embarrassment; but, to the biased understanding of the hostile La Farge, there was something falsely theatrical even in the way Weil cleared his throat.

"Once a grandstander always a grandstander!" he muttered derisively.

"What did you say?" whispered Rogers.

"Nothing," replied La Farge — "just thinking out loud. Listen to what Foxy Issy has to say for himself."

"Well, sir, commissioner," began the accused, "this here thing happens last Thursday, just as Captain Meagher is telling you." He had slipped already into the policeman's trick of detailing a past event in the present tense.

"It's late in the afternoon — round five o'clock I guess — and I'm downstairs in the Detective Bureau alone."

"Alone, you say?" broke in Donohue, emphasizing the word as though the admission scored a point against the man on trial.

"Yes, sir, I'm alone. It happens that everybody else is out and I'm in temporary charge, as you might say. It's getting along toward dark when Patrolman Morgan, who's on duty out in the hall, comes in and says to me there's a woman outside who can't talk English and he can't make out what she wants. So I tells him to bring her in. She comes in. Right away I see she's a Ginney — an Italian," he corrected himself hurriedly. "She's got a child with her — a little boy about two years old."

"Describe this here woman!" ordered Donohue, who loved to drag in details at a trial, not so much for the sake of the details themselves as to show his skill as a cross-examiner.

"Well, sir," complied Weil, "I should say she's about twenty-five years old. It's hard to tell about those Italian women, but I should say she's about twenty-five — or maybe twenty-six. She's got no figure at all and she's dressed poor. But she's got a pretty face — big brown eyes and —"

"That will do," interrupted the deputy commissioner — "that will do for that. I take it you're not qualifyin' here for a beauty expert, Lieutenant Weil!" he added with elaborate sarcasm.

"You asked me about her looks, sir," parried Weil defensively, "and I'm just trying to tell you."

"Proceed! Proceed!" bade Donohue, rumbling his consonants.

"Yes, sir. Well, in regard to this woman: She's talking so fast I can't figure out at first what she's trying to tell me. It's Italian she's talking — or I should say the kind of Italian they talk in parts of Sicily. After a little I begin to see what she's driving at. It seems she's the wife of one Antonio Terranova and her name is Maria Terranova. And after I get her straightened out and going slow she tells me her story."

"Is this here story got a bearin' on the charges pendin'?"

"I think it has. Yes, sir; it helps to explain what happens. As near as I can make out she comes from some small town down round Messina somewhere, and the way she tells it to me, her husband leaves there not long after they're married and comes over here to New York to get work, and when he gets enough money saved up ahead he's going to send back for her. That's near about three years ago. So she stays behind waiting for him, and in about four months after he leaves the baby is born — the same baby that she brings in here to headquarters with her last Thursday. She says neither one of them thinks it'll be long before he can save up money for her passage, but it seems like he has the bad luck. He's sick for a while after he lands, and then when he gets a job in a construction gang the padrone takes the most of what he makes. And just about the time he gets a little saved up some other

Ginney — Italian — in the construction camp steals it off of him.

"So he's up against it, and after a while he gets desperate. So he joins in with a Black Hander gang — amateurs operating up in the Bronx — and the very first trick he helps turn he does well by it. His share is near about a hundred dollars, and he sends her the best part of it to bring her and the baby over. She don't know at the time, though, how he raises all this money — so she tells me. And I think, at that, she's telling the truth — she ain't got sense enough to lie, I think. Anyway it sounds truthful to me — the way she tells it to me here last Thursday night."

"Proceed!" prompted Donohue testily.

"So she takes this here money and buys herself a steerage ticket and comes over here with the baby. That, as near as I can figure out, is about three months ago. She's not seen this husband of hers for going on three years — of course the baby's never seen him. And she figures he'll be at the dock to meet her. But he's not there. But his cousin is there — another Italian from the same town. He gets her through Ellis Island somehow and he takes her up to where he's living — up in the Bronx — and tells her the reason her husband ain't there to meet her. The reason is, he's at Sing Sing, doing four years.

"It seems that after he's sent her this passage money the husband gets to thinking Black Handing is a pretty soft way to make a living, especially compared to day laboring, and he tries to raise a stake single-handed. He writes a Black Hand letter to an Italian grocer he knows has got money laid by, only the grocer is foxy and goes to the Tremont Avenue Station and shows the letter. They rig up a plant and this here Antonio Terranova walks into it. He's caught with the marked bills on him. So just the week before she lands he takes a plea in General Sessions and the judge gives him four years. When she gets to where she's telling me that part of it she starts crying.

"Well, anyway, that's the situation — him up there at Sing Sing doing his four years and her down here in New York with the kid on her hands. And she don't ever see him again, either, because in about three or four weeks — something like that — he's working with a gang in the rock quarry across the river, where they're building the new cell house, and a chunk of slate falls down and kills him and two others."

"Right here and now," interrupted the third deputy commissioner, "I want to know what's all this here stuff got to do with these here charges and specifications?"

"Just a minute, please. I'm coming to that right away, commissioner," protested the accused lieutenant with a sort of glib nervous agility; yet for all of his promising, he paused for a little bit before he continued. And this pause, brief enough as it was, gave the listening La Farge time to discover, with a small inward jar of surprise, that somehow, some way, he was beginning to lose some of his acrid antagonism for Weil; that, by mental processes which as yet he could not exactly resolve into their proper constituents, it was beginning to dribble away from him. And realization came to him, almost with a shock, that the man on the stand was telling the truth. Truth or not, though, the narrative thus far had been commonplace enough — people at headquarters hear the like of it often; and as a seasoned police reporter La Farge's emotions by now should be coated over with a calloused shell inches deep and hard as horn. Trying with half his mind to figure out what it was that had quickened these emotions, he listened all the harder as Weil went on.

"So this here big chunk of rock or slate or whatever it was falls on him and the two others and kills them. Not knowing where to send the body, they bury it up there at Sing Sing, and she never sees him again, living or dead. But here just a few days ago it seems she picks up, from overhearing some of the other Italians talking, that we've got such a thing as a Rogues' Gallery down here at headquarters and that her husband's picture is liable to be in it. So that's why she's here. She's found her way here somehow and she asks me won't I" — he caught himself — "won't the police please give her her husband's picture out of the gallery."

"And for why did she want that?" rumbled Donohue.

"That's what I asks her myself. It seems she's got no shame about it at all. She tells me she wants to hang on to it until she can get the money to have it enlarged into a big picture, and then she's going to keep it — till the bambino — that's Italian for baby, commissioner, you know — till the baby grows up, so he can see what his dead father looked like."

Now of a sudden La Farge knew — or thought he knew — why his interest had stirred in him a minute before. Instinctively his reporter's sixth sense had scented a good news story before the real point of the story had come out, even. A curious little silence had fallen on the half-lighted, almost empty big room. Only the voice of Weil broke this silence:

"Of course, commissioner, I tries to explain to her what the circumstances are. I tells her that, in the first place, on account of the mayor's orders about cutting down the gallery having gone into effect, it's an even bet her husband's picture ain't there anyhow — that it's most likely been destroyed; and in the second place, even if it is there, I tells her I've got no right to be giving it to her without an order from somebody higher up. But either she can't understand or she won't. I guess my being in uniform makes her think I'm running the whole department, and she won't seem to listen to what I says.

"She cries and she carries on worse than ever, and begs and begs me to give it to her. I guess you know how excitable those Italian women can be, especially when they are Sicilians. Anyhow, commissioner, after a lot of that sort of thing I tells her to wait where she is for a minute. I leaves her and I goes across into the Bertillon room, where the pictures are, and I looks up this here Antonio Terranova. I forget his number now and I don't know how it is he comes to be overlooked when we're cleaning out the gallery; but he's there all right, full face and side view, with his gallery number in big white figures on his chest. And, commissioner, he's a pretty tolerable tough-looking Ginney." The witness checked an inclination to grin. "I takes a slant at his picture, and I can't make up my own mind which way he'll look the worst enlarged into a crayon portrait — full face or side view. I can still hear her crying outside the door. She's crying harder than ever.

"I puts the picture back, and I goes out to where she is and tries to argue with her. It's no use. She goes down on her knees and holds the baby up, and tells me it ain't for her sake she's asking this — it's for the bambino. And she calls on a lot of Italian saints that I never even heard the names of some of them before — and so on, like that. It's pretty tough.

"She's such a stupid, ignorant thing you can't help from feeling sorry for her — nobody could." He hesitated a moment as though seeking for words of explanation and extenuation that were not in his regular vocabulary. "I got kids of my own, commissioner," he said suddenly, and stopped dead short for a moment. "I'm no Italian, but I got kids of my own!" he repeated, as though the fact constituted a defense.

"Well, well — what happened then?" The deputy commissioner's frosty voice seemed to have frozen so hard it had a crack in it. And now then the Semitic face of Weil twisted into a grin that was more than shamefaced — it was downright sheepish.

"Why, then," he said, "when I comes back out of the Bertillon room the second time she goes back down on her knees again and she says to me — of course she ain't expected to know what my religion is — maybe that explains it, commissioner — she says to me that all her life — every morning and every night — she's going to pray to the Blessed Virgin for me. That's what she says anyway. So I just lets it go at that."

He halted as though he were through.

"Then do I understand that, without an order from any superior authority, you gave this here woman certain property belonging to the Police Department?" Old Donohue's voice was gruffer than common, even. He whetted his talon forefinger on the desk top.

"Yes, sir," owned up the Jew. "There's nobody there but just us two. And I don't know how Captain Meagher comes to find the picture is gone and that it was me took it — but it's true, commissioner. She goes away kissing it and holding it to the breast of her clothes — that Rogues' Gallery picture! Yes, sir; I gives it to her."

The third deputy commissioner's gold-banded right arm was shoved out, with all the lean fingers upon the hand at the far end of it widely extended. He spoke, and something in his throat — a hard lump perhaps — husked his brogue and made his r's roll out like dice.

"Lieutenant Weil," he said, "I congratulate you! You're guilty!"

THE END